HOSPICE

HOSPICE

Gregory Howard

TUSCALOOSA

FC2 is an imprint of The University of Alabama Press
Inquiries about reproducing material from this work should be addressed
to the University of Alabama Press.

Book Design: Illinois State University's English Department's Publications
    Unit; Codirectors: Steve Halle and Jane L. Carman; Assistant Director:
    Danielle Duvick; Production Assistant: Taylor Williams
Cover Design: Lou Robinson
Typeface: Garamond

⊗

The paper on which this book is printed meets the minimum
requirements of American National Standard for Information
Sciences—Permanence of Paper for Printed Library Materials, ANSI
Z39.48–1984

Library of Congress Cataloging-in-Publication Data
Howard, Gregory, 1974-
Hospice / Gregory Howard.
    pages cm
    ISBN 978-1-57366-051-8 (pbk. : alk. paper)—ISBN 978-1-57366-855-
2 (ebook)
    1. Hospice care—Fiction. 2. Nursing—Vocational guidance. 3. Isolation
(Hospital care)—Fiction. I. Title.
    PS3608.O9223 2015
    813'.6—dc23
                            2014035853

"Who's there?"

Hamlet, Act I, sc. I

For my parents
and my sister

HOSPICE

By the side of a road, the boy and girl are playing. The road goes on for miles in either direction. No houses are visible. No buildings at all. It is just the road. The road, the meadow, the woods. And, in the distance, the sea. The smell of it. The boy and girl each have wispy, mud-colored hair of equal length. If not for a slight height difference, they might be identical, interchangeable. The girl has a sharp rock in her left hand. She places the tip against her brother's forehead, right between the eyes. Ok, she says. This is going to pinch a little. Get it out, he says. Just get it out. She begins to push the rock into his flesh. Wait, he says. She pulls the rock away and fixes him with her eyes. You forgot to say: in case of accidental death is there anything I wish to express to my loved ones. She looks at him for a moment. He is serious, concerned. She rubs the rock with her thumb and forefinger; caresses it. In case of accidental death, she says, her voice calm, low, is there anything you wish to express to your loved ones? He looks down for a moment as if considering the dirt. In the woods around them birds skitter and call. No, he says finally. She quickly thrusts the rock into his head. Blood trickles down the bridge of his nose. She steps back and peers into her hands. Well? he says with a concerned look. Her hands open to reveal a small violet. His face transforms. I told you so, he says triumphantly. She hands him the flower and the rock. Now it's my turn, she says, smiling.

Part I

Then she found herself caring for the memory of an old woman's dog.

Of course this wasn't how Lucy first understood the position. At first it seemed like any other job. She went out in the afternoons, the woman said, as she led Lucy from room to room, to run errands and occasionally play some bridge and needed someone to look after her dog, Popsicle, who really wasn't much trouble now that he was getting on. The job was easy. Feed Popsicle at three and let him out into the backyard afterwards to do his business. That was it. That was the whole job. The food was kept in an opaque plastic bin underneath the sink, the treats in a shiny blue jar with the word "woof" inscribed in wobbly black letters. There was a number for—God forbid—the emergency vet and the thermostat had to be kept at seventy degrees at all times. It helps with Popsicle's bones, the woman said, the corners of her mouth curled with delicate sadness.

While the woman talked, Lucy looked around for the dog. Every time they entered a room she expected to find him there, waiting for them. But each room was empty, dogless. The house was dim, darkened against the afternoon's insistent light by dusty blinds, but it was also small. Realistically, there weren't many places for a dog to hide. Especially a dog the size of Popsicle. Because Popsicle—it turned out—was a fat brown lab with a square head and an enthusiastic, bewildered countenance. There were pictures of him everywhere. On every wall and every desk, on every bureau and table there he was—looking happy and maybe a little bit deranged. In quite a few of the pictures he wore unimaginative holiday outfits—Popsicle the joyful elf, the bow-tied rabbit, the kindly witch. A dog like that, she thought, would be hard to miss. Certainly he wouldn't be cowering behind the credenza. It seemed to her as if that very instant Popsicle should be bounding around them disruptively, or at least following them absently with a slight and amiable wag of his tail. But the whole house was quiet. The house was still.

The situation, Lucy felt, was both curious and a little bit alarming. She had found the job through this website that specialized in local animal needs. Here, as everywhere, there was a lot of need. On the website people bought and sold animals; they solicited advice and considered counsel; they reverently described their own animals' wonderful, idiosyncratic behavior; they posted pictures with funny captions. It was a community dedicated to the holy mysteries of animal companionship and so the people who hung out there, while mostly sincere and kind-hearted, tended to be more than a little erratic.

Like, once, for example, she answered an ad to care for a sweet and loving bulldog from a woman who called herself Nancy. When she arrived at Nancy's house, however, she found herself watching a pit bull eat the foam out of an old orange couch.

That's not a bulldog, she said.

My precious little Buster? Nancy said. Don't be ridiculous!

For one, Lucy said, a bulldog is smaller, I think.

Are you calling me a liar? Nancy said. Are you calling *Buster* a liar? He has papers. He has credentials.

I'm ok with it, she said. I can still take care of him. I just want to be on the same page.

Nancy paced in circles and wrung her hands while Buster continued with the couch.

You're sick, Nancy hissed. You're one of *those*. We don't need you. *Buster* doesn't need you. Isn't that right, she asked the dog, little Buster-man?

This was typical, Lucy thought later. People wanted animals but they didn't really know what to do with them. They considered them, but only on their own terms.

He's a sleeper, the old woman was saying, a cuddler.

The tour had ended and they were back in the living room. The old woman was buttoning up her tan mackintosh and pulling on thin cotton gloves. Popsicle had still failed to appear, but this didn't seem to perturb the woman much at all. She was getting ready to go; she had places to be.

Occasionally, he can be a *little* fussy, the woman said. She smoothed out her coat and grabbed her handbag.

But if you don't look at him *directly* in the eyes, she continued, you should be just fine.

Lucy glanced around the room. She was sure that now, at last, the dog would materialize. He would arrive with haste to salute his departing mistress, to offer up a bit of himself—memory, image, animal soul—for his owner to carry forward, like armor, into the day's dull assault. The woman adjusted her gloves; she applied some lipstick. Still no Popsicle. With the dog neglecting even this basic duty, Lucy didn't really know what to think. Maybe, she decided, he was in the back yard or napping in a closet. Maybe he was underneath a bush somewhere, gnawing on something rotten. She felt for a moment a little giddy about what would unfold after the woman left and shut the door behind her, as if all the oxygen had been momentarily sucked from the room, as if she were about to leap from the high wall of a quarry into the cool blackness of whatever lurked below.

Then at the front door, just before her exit, the old woman turned to the empty couch and waved at it.

Goodbye Popsicle! the woman said with tender enthusiasm.

That was when Lucy realized what her duties really were.

A few weeks later she was sitting on the plastic-slip-covered couch at Popsicle's house, dreaming up the day's adventure. Usually it wasn't much. Popsicle chased a squirrel in the back yard. Popsicle added an extra hop to his treat dance. Little things. Dog things. They weren't difficult to conceive. Still, they gave the woman so much pleasure. *My Popsicle?* the woman would say with disbelief. *My little guy?! I wish I could have been there to see it!* Then she would give Lucy some money and apologize. *It's not enough,* the woman always said. *But it's given with profound appreciation.* At first, Lucy wasn't really sure what to do with the money. It seemed wrong to get paid for helping a senile woman pretend to have a dog. Like maybe she was conning her out of her pension or something. But on the other hand, the woman was happy. Was that so bad? Everyone believed in at least one impossible thing. A dog seemed inoffensive somehow. She put the money in a jar and placed it in the back of her closet.

Today, though, she was trying to think of a different story. She wasn't sure quite what to conjure up except that it should be more memorable. The woman was clearly becoming bored and restless. The last time Lucy was there, the woman had listened half-heartedly to the day's story and then wandered off down the hall to her bedroom. How about that, the woman had said without enthusiasm. Lucy thought maybe the woman was going to get her payment out of her bureau, out of the top drawer, where, Lucy knew, she kept her spending money, bills and change and the bills sorted into envelopes of different sizes and hues, hidden underneath a layer of baggy silk underwear, so she sat on the couch and waited. The woman, however, did not come back out. She just stayed there in her bedroom doing God knows what. The door remained slightly ajar. The long hallway was dim and kind of foreboding. The air-conditioning droned malignantly. Lucy walked to the bedroom door and peered in. The old woman in full dress—navy slacks, flats, buttoned up tan mackintosh, cotton cloves—lay on her back, eyes closed, her arms and legs spread out as if she had fallen asleep in the midst of making a snow angel. Her chest rose and fell. Her breathing was raspy, thin. See you Tuesday, Lucy had called out softly and let herself out.

She got up and walked around a bit. The woman's house was tidy in the way that old women's houses generally were. The counters were spotless and the cabinets spare and organized. The carpet was cream-colored and soft, replete with vacuum lines. In the bathrooms there were fragrant little soaps and bowls with potpourri. The house didn't lend itself to stories, that was for sure.

Then suddenly the doorbell rang. She looked out the big picture window. At the front door a boy and a girl were waiting. The girl was tall and thin with long, wispy, dishwater hair.

The boy was squat and chubby. He was wearing a powder blue surgical mask.

Lucy opened the door.

Yes? she said.

Our mom said we could have a cookie, the boy said. His voice was high-pitched and clear despite the mask.

For a moment she didn't now what to say. The boy and the girl just stood there.

That's nice, she said, finally.

She did! She said it! the boy exclaimed. I heard her say it! He was getting agitated. His eyes were wide open and his pupils dilated.

The woman who lives here, the girl explained, sometimes she gives us cookies

Oh, Lucy said.

They're in the kitchen, the girl said.

Ok, she said.

They're the sandwich kind, the girl said.

Come in, she said.

At the kitchen table, the boy stuffed cookies underneath his mask and chewed noisily. The mask had a variety of stains on it. Some deep red.

There's an outbreak at school, the girl explained. Her arms were pale and seemed fragile. They were full of freckles and light scratches. So I have to stay home because he does.

Nuh-uh, the boy said, his mouth full of cookies.

He has a delicate immune system, the girl said. That's what the doctor says.

Don't be a jerk, the boy grumbled.

You don't be a jerk, she said. *I'm* not the one who's lying.

It's my one weakness, the boy admitted. But I make up for it with my many superpowers.

He shoved another cookie underneath his mask. The mask moved erratically as he ate. It resembled a paper bag in which a small frantic animal had been trapped.

Eventually the boy finished off the box. It didn't take long. Then they all sat around the table quietly. The table was a deep burnished wood with a plastic mat on top. There was nothing really to say about it, Lucy felt. Nothing to say about any of it. The table, the cupboards, the couch. But something, she thought, had to be said. Always, there was that. Basic conversation. It made her anxious. Not to mention basic conversation with children, which often started with such promise, such dizzy possibility, but usually ended in monotony or tears. She thought she should be better at it. Unplanned objects give us a glimpse of the inner order, her brother once told her. Her brother.

And soon, she knew, the woman would be home. How would she reckon with this? Two strange children and one wearing a mask. Lucy tried to think how Popsicle's adventure might involve all of them, but the very thought of it seemed to dissolve into half-sketched shapes and unrealized movements. No, she thought. It was a bad idea. The woman clearly had enough on her plate. She was sensitive to the slightest disturbance of schedule. Really, what had to happen was that the children had to leave.

She tried appealing to the girl, who was clearly in charge, giving her a look of pleading and exasperation.

You have something in your eye, the girl said.

The boy left the table and got up on the counter and went through the cupboards.

Lucy sighed and slumped in her seat a little. It was happening again.

There's nothing here, he said.

Generally speaking, Lucy told him, that's the case. It's probably worth getting used to.

What's matzo? he asked. He had dug out a box out from way back in the cabinet.

It's a cracker made without yeast, the girl said. For some cultures it represents redemption and freedom.

Ick, he said. They're terrible.

They're not really suitable for childlike appetites, Lucy told him. But some people find them very nourishing.

He got down from the counter and sat himself back at the table. Jittery and plump, he looked around the room with scattered expectation, humming to himself. Across the table, Marinella was still with lassitude and boredom. They had arrived like a sudden cloud of insects at dusk and now here they were, thwarted, sure, but still attendant, waiting for something to happen, some wayward miracle. A cookie, a kiss, a revelation.

Listen, said Lucy, after thinking it through. Do you guys want to see something?

What is it? the boy asked warily.

It's a secret, she said.

Like pirate treasure? he asked, now a bit excitedly.

Kind of, she said.

Is it a dead body?

But if you agree to see it, she said, then you have to also agree to go home afterwards.

The boy looked doubtful.

I don't see why that's any kind of a bargain, the girl said. Carol likes us. She let's us do what we whatever we want.

Carol? she said.

The woman that lives here? the girl said disdainfully.

Oh, she said. Right. Carol. Well, you know, do whatever you want. It's the only offer on the table.

The boy looked into the cupboards and then at his sister. Please, he said. Can we?

The girl rolled her eyes.

They left the house and Lucy led them through the neighborhood. The boy held her hand. She hadn't asked him to, he just did it.

Her name is Marinella, he said. Mine's Tim. Marinella means little sea. Tim just means Tim.

He sounded sad about this.

Tim's hand was warm and sticky. It squirmed restlessly in her loose grasp. The girl trailed behind them.

This part of the neighborhood had the look of having once enjoyed some glamour. The houses were all someone's idea of the future, now past. They were low to the ground and comprised of exotic geometric shapes and soft rounded corners. Giant, dying trees lined the street. Their rotting branches hung low.

Where are we going? Tim said.

She doesn't know, Marinella said. She's just taking us wherever.

She knows! Tim shrieked. She knows! He looked at her anxiously. You know, right?

Lucy squeezed his hand reassuringly.

They walked a few more blocks in silence and then turned into an alley. Overgrown lilac bushes and sprouting elms formed a considerable thicket.

We'll have to crawl from here, she said.

This is it? Marinella asked.

I know what this is, Tim stated. It's an entrance. It's an opening into a mysterious realm filled with magic annnd... maybe candy. Am I right?

He looked at Lucy with giddy expectation.

It's something like that, she said

The thicket was dense. Lucy took the lead, breaking off little branches where she could, but still the shrubs snagged her clothes and scratched at her skin. Did they draw blood? Will they? Behind her she could hear Tim chattering. What if there's an angry gnome, she heard him say. You're such a nerd, Marinella said. You're a nerd! Tim retorted. Shhh, she told them. Shhhh. The lilac bushes were all in bloom and their scent was cloying and intense. It sent her out of her body. I am the one who wants them, she thought. Underneath them, the ground was soft and wet. They crawled on their hands and knees and sometimes their bellies. She felt it cool and clotted, the mud, smearing itself on her skin, finding furrows, lines, nests, and the rocks sharp against the soft hollows of her palms, poking there, probing, insisting on entry. They crawled past yards with cut lawns and sensible furniture. Her breath was a pulse and a din. The lilacs, the mud, the rocks. She crawled and crawled and crawled. Then she stopped.

She stopped in front of a chain link fence and maneuvered herself into a squat. Tim and Marinella squeezed in next to her. Above them a tangled bush provided a low canopy. In front of them was a medium-sized yard and the back of a house. There was nothing distinctive about either. The yard was barely a yard at all. It was a small rectangle of patchily mown grass abutting cracked cement patio without furniture. There were cigarette butts scattered everywhere. On one end of the patio was a red plastic rocking horse without a discernible mouth, stranded and aloof, surveying his empty kingdom.

What is this place? Tim asked

Just wait, she said.

He shifted impatiently next to her.

After a few minutes a horn sounded and the cellar door opened. Out of it marched about twenty men. They were all young and each one wore bright blue loose-fitting pants and matching V-neck T-shirts. Upon exiting the door and climbing the stairs, they abruptly turned right and followed the fence to its post and then turned again. They marched in this way along the chain link fence circling the patchy yard until they reached the cellar door again. They were men of different builds and haircuts but they all wore the same vacant yet serious expressions.

Who are they? Marinella said, entranced.

They're patients, she said.

Patients? Marinella said.

People not well enough to live around other people so they live together, to the side of other people.

Tim adjusted his mask and scooted back a little.

Are they dangerous? he asked.

For a moment Lucy didn't reply.

Probably not, she said eventually.

The men had broken up into different groups. Some were playing cards in the grass. Some were doing jumping jacks. Others were doing nothing at all, just staring at things unseen. Whatever those men did, they did in silence.

They're wonderful, Marinella said, breathlessly.

The next day Tim and Marinella came over again. This time Tim was no longer wearing his mask. Marinella, however, was wearing a dull yellow swimsuit. It wasn't particularly warm out. Thin gray clouds hung low in a hazy sky. Marinella's belly protruded defiantly. Her skin looked pale and waxen.

There aren't any cookies, Lucy said.

We don't want cookies, Marinella said.

Yes we do, said Tim.

We want something else, said Marinella.

Lucy looked at them, defiant, needy.

What's that, Lucy said.

We can't tell you out here, Marinella said.

Because it's a secret, Tim said with excitement. A real one. And you have to tell secrets in the dark when you're all sitting in a circle and holding hands, right Mari?

He looked at his sister with expectation. But Marinella looked only at Lucy.

Fine, Lucy said. Come on in.

Inside, in Carol's dim kitchen, they sat around the table again.

What we want, said Marinella, is for you to take us back to the place. We tried going ourselves but we couldn't find it. I don't know why we couldn't find it but we couldn't.

I know! Tim squealed, bouncing in his seat a little. It's like I said: it's magical and magical places always have entrances that move!

Don't be stupid, Tim, said Marinella.

Tim fell back into his chair and slumped down. His eyes began to glisten.

We can't go today, Lucy said.

Why not?

Because, she said. They don't come out today.

Why not?

I don't know, she said. They just don't.

Marinella looked upset and skeptical. Tim snuffled and played with the drawstrings of his shorts.

But, Marinella said. Then how did you know they would be out yesterday?

I didn't, said Lucy. But I thought it was worth a try.

This was true. The men's movements adhered to an unseen clock. She had spent some time watching them, these men. She had gauged what passed for rituals and routines. She had observed them in the bushes, from behind the fence, and she had watched them from across the street. She had kept notes. The notes said: not him, not him. Not her brother.

But the meager truth wasn't a solace. Marinella looked clearly exasperated. She kicked at the legs of the table. They all sat in silence.

We could do something else, Lucy offered, eventually.

Like what, said Marinella.

You could tell us a story, Tim said.

I could do that, Lucy said.

She took them into the backyard. Here Popsicle took his naps in the sun, sniffed at the mums and, sometimes, barked at the squirrels that ran up and down the big tree. At times Lucy thought she could almost see him lying there in the thin, patchy grass, brown and shadowy.

They sat in the shade. Tim curled up next to her and put his head in her lap. Marinella sat several feet away.

She thought for a while and then started.

Once, she said, there was a girl with nine brothers.

That's terrible, Marinella said.

However, the girl didn't know she had nine brothers, she continued, because they had all disappeared just after she was born. One day they were out in the fields with their father and they just vanished.

Because of a witch's curse? Tim said.

Exactly, she said.

Once she grew up a little she began to have suspicions that something was not right. There was something unwholesome about her parents' behavior. They loved her too much. Like there was a hole at the bottom of their loving. So one day she confronted them. She said, I have lived in this house all my life and yet for me it does not feel like a home. It has always felt like something is missing or has been misplaced. What is it that I have done? What do I need to do? As soon as she spoke these words, her mother broke down crying and her father took on a pained and weary look. Sit down, he said. And they all sat around the kitchen table. He said, Here is the thing we have always known and never wanted to say.

And now because of our secrecy and our desires we must do this thing, the thing we never, ever wanted to do. He sighed. When your mother was pregnant, her father said, I traveled deep into the forest to make a wish at the wishing tree. I had but one wish. I would do anything to have a little girl. At the time, your brothers were causing me much pain. Instead of working, they were always playing in the trees or running off into town to cause havoc. Their idleness ruined the crops and we lost friends and neighbors due to their excitability and taste for casual violence. A little baby girl seemed the antidote to these troubles. A beautiful, docile baby girl. So at the time I made the wish at the wishing tree, I was thinking about your brothers and how much trouble they caused me and how I wished, at times, they would just stay in town or in those trees and leave us alone to welcome our new and precious joy. I made my wish and I paid my price. For a while nothing happened. Your mother's pregnancy was like all pregnancies and the boys were still the boys. But then right after you were born it happened. Right in front of our eyes. It happened. Your brothers disappeared into thin air. One minute, they were there, around the supper table, arguing and stealing bread. The next, the room was empty. It is all my fault, her father said. Wishing is a dangerous business. However, out of it we got you. And we will never let you go.

Despite her father's protestations the girl knew that she was the one responsible for her brothers' disappearance. After all, it was her very own birth that caused it! So, one night, she escaped out of the window and traveled to the wishing tree. She brought with her one jug of water, a half a loaf of bread, and a mirror. When she found the wishing tree, she said, Tree, how can I bring back my brothers? The Tree said, Before I tell you, you must give me some of your blood. She looked around for a moment and then decided to smash the mirror and use it. She smashed it against the tree and took one of the shards and cut her hand. She let it bleed onto the Tree. With every drop, the tree brightened and shuddered. After it had finished feeding, the Tree said to her, To bring your brothers back you must have four adventures and complete them. But you won't know that you've had them until after they've occurred. Only then will your brothers return. So she went off, traveling around the country. Nothing adventurous happened on these travels. She met a man with one arm, but he was not a warlock. She saw a waterfall, but it was not an entrance. Everything was exactly what it appeared to be. Everything was a disappointment. Finally, she ended up waiting on weary travelers at a run-down inn. Hustling between the throaty calls and grubby hands of the tavern's patrons, she felt as if she had reached some kind of ending. She had aged terribly, she thought, and wondered if during her sojourn she had done something incorrectly. What had the tree said about incorrect paths? About shadow that was merely shadow and light that was merely light? She couldn't recall. Sometimes when she looked in the mirror she saw something behind her face that stared back at her with malice. Eventually she grew so tired she decided it was time to return home. Adventures or no adventures. Brothers or no brothers. She returned the way she had come and when she walked in the door she saw, to her surprise, her nine brothers sitting quietly at the table with her parents. They were eating bowls of terrible-smelling soup. Everyone stared at her, shocked. Where have you been? her parents said. I've been out searching the wide country for my brothers, she said. What are you talking about? her parents said. My brothers, she said. They disappeared and I went in search of them and had adventures until they could be saved. And now they are saved so I must have had my adventures. Your brothers were never missing, her parents said. Your brothers have been here all along. It was you that was missing. You have been gone for three days. And since you have nothing but lies for explanations you can go to your room. They sent her to bed without supper. Her brothers eyed her suspiciously and never trusted her a day in her life. But she knew what she had done and how she had saved them.

The whole time she told this story Lucy didn't look at the children. She looked at the house. In particular she looked at a brick wall and a small window. Through the window she could see the bathroom, which was tiled in mauve. Whenever Carol returned she conducted herself immediately to the bathroom where she refreshed the potpourri and checked the medicine cabinet for theft. Only then did she steady herself for conversation and payment. In the window there was a small porcelain cat, whose head peered out at the backyard, surveying its unreachable kingdom. It looked frightened. Now, however, with the story finished, she looked at Tim and Marinella and found they were sleeping. They were curled up and dreaming.

Hey, Lucy said. Wake up.

She shook them both gently but firmly.

What is it? Marinella said.

It's over, she said.

That's it? Tim asked.

That's it, she said.

She walked them home. Both children were wobbly with sleep. Marinella led the way, but barely. They seemed to be merely wandering around, just coasting through the dormant yards, family after family. Finally, however, they came to a red brick two-story house with an overgrown front yard. In front of the house, a woman wearing a navy business suit and black high heels was getting into a boxy green station wagon. When she saw them she got out and put her hand on her wide hips.

Oh my goodness, the woman said. I was worried sick.

She called the children to her and hugged them tightly into her blazered chest. Her movement was forceful and brusque. After she was done hugging them, she shooed the two straight into the house. Right inside, she said. Then she turned around.

My goodness, the woman said. Thank you so much. Those two, I mean, sometimes I don't even know where to begin. Here, she said. She rustled around in her purse and pulled out some bills, a little change, and held it out in front of her, crumpled in her hand, an offering.

Oh no, said Lucy. I couldn't.

Of course you could, the woman said. You're just choosing not to.

She smiled. Her teeth were a shining cosmetic white.

It was really nothing.

There's no such thing as nothing, the woman said and laughed. It was a loud and raspy laugh.

Why don't you come in? she said. I'll fix you something.

I'm fine, said Lucy. I should be going.

You're famished, the woman said. Just look at you. Plus you're practically inside already.

The woman turned and walked breezily into the house, leaving the door wide open for her. Lucy peered into the house. The hallway was dark and long and at the end of it was the kitchen.

In the kitchen the woman was bustling around, putting things in various cupboards. She pulled out a bottle of scotch, filled a tumbler with ice, and sat down at the round kitchen table to fix herself a drink.

You want one? the woman asked.

No thanks, said Lucy.

Personally speaking, the woman said. I don't know how you can get through the day without it.

She took a sip of hers and emitted an involuntary whimper of pleasure

Liquid meditation, the woman said. Are you sure you don't want any?

She took the bottle and refilled the glass.

I'm good, said Lucy.

Your life, the woman proclaimed.

She took another drink and then placed the glass on the counter with care.

Ok, the woman said. Listen. I just had an idea. A brilliant idea. It's really great. How would you, she said, like a job?

What? said Lucy

A job, the woman said. J. O. B.

That's ok, Lucy said.

Don't be a simp, the woman said.

I've already got a job.

Nonsense, the woman replied. The whole point of having a job is to get a better job. And *this*, she waved her drink around in the air as if she show off the kitchen, is a better job.

She took a sip.

The kids told me they found you at kooky Carol's, she continued. Do you think there are really prospects there? I mean: what can you actually learn? How do you improve yourself? I like Carol. We all do. But what I suspect is that you're doing the doggy paddle in the big wide ocean. That's what my Daddy used to say about ruts you don't even know you're in. So what I'm offering you is a chance to shake things up for yourself. Get yourself a new track. A new destination. How does that sound?

Lucy shrugged noncommittally.

Look, the woman said, obviously these kids need supervision. I thought Marinella was up to the task. But clearly she lacks focus. Just wandering around the neighborhood in her bathing suit, knocking on strange doors. Good lord! It's enough to make you fall over in your chair. I mean: Can you even imagine who might have found them? It makes me sick to think about it. So more than anything what I'm really asking for is a little help, a little charity. But one you'll get paid for, she said brightly.

Now, here are things you need to know: One, Tim's a bit of a sissy. Which you wouldn't expect given his, you know, size. But there's only so much a mother can do, right? I can't go out there and rough it up for him, can I? I blame his father. That man never knew a conflict he wouldn't shrink from. Just getting him to order more bread at a restaurant was like I'd asked him to shout slurs in Harlem. He'd sit there and squirm in his seat, literally squirm. Finally, I'd just have to grab the bull by the horns. But let me tell you: you can only grab so many horns before you become the bull, you know what I'm saying? I guess it was doomed from the very start.

The woman sighed.

From the front of the house Lucy could hear Marinella saying, Stop it! And Tim saying, You stop it!

Never choose a man based on the fit of his jeans, she admonished. That's the lesson. Anyway this is important information to have, she continued, because, Two—she held up two fingers unsteadily—Marinella will probably pick on him. It's kind of a recent thing. She used to adore him. After he was born she called him her Baby Lump. Can you even imagine that? The things kids come up with. I swear. Sometime I look at those two and marvel. I just marvel. I'd think they were from another planet if I hadn't seen them squirm right out of me.

The woman paused to consider her drink and then partake of it.

These days Marinella can be sullen, she said. And weird. I mean don't get me wrong. On any given day that girl can light up a room. It's just that those particular days don't come but once a month now. It's like she's getting her reverse period or something.

The woman sighed again and took another, long drink.

That's about it, she said. How's it sound?

Look, said Lucy.

Oh, the woman said, you also need to keep notes on what the neighbor to the south does.

I'm…

That bitch is always up to something, the woman said. I'm pretty sure she's slowly moving my fence over to get more room for her roses. She's moving it in centimeters. She thinks I don't notice. But I notice. Part of your job is to notice too. Can you handle that?

She looked at Tim and Marinella in the other room. They were sitting Indian-style in front of the television. It was only the two of them, it seemed. No other friends, no father, the mother and her manias. Always that. On the television, a hyper boy and his magical dog were having absurd adventures in a benign universe. Tim and Marinella's faces were wide with anticipation.

Sure, she said.

That evening when Lucy returned home the girls, were holding a séance in her room. The girls were the group of young women who lived with her in this big, sagging Victorian. The house had many rooms and each room contained one of the girls. They looked the same and dressed the same and spoke to each other in soft words that were sometimes hard to understand.

For fun sometimes they would put on puppet shows in the large circular den on the first floor. The puppet show was always the same. In it a man was walking with confidence through a haunted wood. He was redoubtable in his bearing and choice of costume. These woods did not scare him. After all, he was a man who has walked through other woods, through deeper and darker and more haunted woods. In other words, he was a man of purpose. And because his purpose lay beyond these woods, the trees around him, as he walked, became to him nothing more than background, as if he was not in a forest at all, as if the trees had been painted hastily on flimsy canvas. He walked and walked. But then suddenly he stopped. He stopped in front of a tree and from it broke a thin branch; he stripped the branch and waved it in front of him with pleasure, listening to it whip through the air. Why did he do this? The branch was too small to be a walking stick and he had no need of a switch. He caressed it gently, his lovely branch, and his gentleness resembled a kind of desperate pawing. But then just as quickly as he had procured the branch, he dropped it and, without a backward glance, continued on his way. The sound of the woods was pleasant to him now; the light gentle, alluring. His journey now felt as if it were nothing more than an afternoon ramble. Later there would be tea and small sandwiches. But meanwhile, unbeknownst to him, inside the trunk of the now mutilated tree, the now mutilated woman he once loved cried out in anguish. He had wounded her once again. She had come to him transformed in his hour of direst need but all he can do is wound. Why hadn't she foreseen this? The man continued gamely on. He whistled. He left the woods and found himself another landscape, another object to desire. It was only after he was far from the forest that the tree began to bleed.

Lucy wasn't supposed to see these shows and she knew she wasn't supposed to see them because the girls would stop talking when she passed them in the hallways. But she watched anyway. She sat on the stairs and watched as the puppets moved in discordant jumps like something was chewing on their nerves. They had waxen, implacable faces. They seemed sinister.

Tonight though they were in her room. The girls. They were sitting there in a kind of oblong circle amongst a smattering of candles and whispers. They were talking to the dead.

Oh, one said, after Lucy had walked through the door, we thought you'd gone to visit your family.

My family? Lucy said.

Or a faraway friend, the girl offered.

What are you talking about? Lucy said.

For a while they looked at each other, she and everyone else, with slight mutual suspicion.

Things have gone missing from the house, someone said. Little things. Knives, drinking glasses, shoes. Those kinds of things. We considered our options and a séance seemed the best course of action.

You decided to do it here, Lucy said. In my room.

Cardinal points are important, the girl said. She had a book and held it in front of her with an air of solemn authority.

Oh, she said.

I thought we were doing an exorcism, one said.

As if, another said.

You don't expel someone before a certainty can be established, the girl with the book responded.

Yeah, the girl next to her chimed in. I mean: what if it's friendly?

I don't know. Is there such a thing? Like would they return if they were benevolent? Do benevolent things come back?

Do benevolent things come back? someone said in diminishing, mocking tones.

Don't be a bitch, someone else said.

They don't return, another explained. They just don't leave. Even when you want them to. They don't get that you want them to.

I lived in a place with one once, one girl said softly. I would come home and find the appliances going. A different one each time. Like one day the blender and the next, the coffee maker.

How lovely. It's like it was greeting you. Like it was telling you it was happy to see you.

That's a bit naïve, don't you think?

The landlord came over and looked at the wiring and said everything was just fine. Nothing wrong with the wiring. There's never anything wrong with the wiring, he said. He was sad about it. It turned out that this had been happening for a while, ever since his grandmother died in that apartment. Died right there in the kitchen.

Shouldn't they have to tell you that, when you're looking at a place? I think that's something you should know.

Listen, said the girl with the book.

She died out of loneliness. The grandmother. Or at least that was what the landlord thought. He had lived there and taken care of her as long as he could and when he couldn't anymore, when his grandmother had become so sick that she required professional care, he bought the place next door and moved there. He had a wife and child, he said. They needed the space. They needed a life of their own. And he could still be the same person he always was, just right next door. But the grandmother thought it was a terrible slight, unforgiveable, and didn't talk to him ever again. He would knock on her door and she would stand there and not answer. He could hear her wheezing through the door. She wasn't a hard woman, he said. Just scared. His mother had left both of them to fend for themselves. Just ran off one day with a blackjack dealer. And he was all she had and he wasn't enough. Later though, his mother came back and lived there for a while but then she died too. But he knew that the ghost was his grandmother. He could feel her in her anger and her love. His mother, she hadn't like it enough to stay the first time. Why would she stay now? Plus anyway, he said, the time had passed for people to be ghosts. Now, after death, they were just fleeting thoughts.

That's fucked up.

I don't know. I think it's kind of beautiful.

I guess people are as unforgiving in death as they are in life, said Lucy.

No one looked at her.

It was nice, the girl telling the story said. It was nice. To feel like I wasn't alone.

But now you have us!

Listen, someone pleaded. Are we going to do this?

Why not? another said.

Everyone held hands.

C'mon, a girl said. Now that you're here you have to be a part.

Lucy sat down and entered the circle. A girl on each side of her took her hands. Their hands were cool and smooth.

The girl with the book told them to empty their minds.

Lucy tried to empty her mind but it didn't seem to work.

Ok spirit, the girl with the book said, we know you're there and we know what you've been doing.

Is it a good idea to talk to it like that?

I think you're supposed to say "Oh spirit." Otherwise it won't respond, another said.

Shhh, someone admonished.

Oh spirit, someone said.

Shhhh.

Listen. We don't want to hurt you. We don't even want to know who you are, or why you're here. Honestly we don't care. We just want to stop taking our things. Stop taking them and putting them in strange places.

And stop inhabiting our rooms when we're not there, one chimed in.

We're not unreasonable, the girl with the book said. We're willing to compromise.

Lucy imagined the spirit there listening, silent and bemused. Were ghosts logical? Could they be reasoned with? Or were they more like animals? Like silent animals watching and waiting. To her they seemed more like animals.

Does anyone feel cold? the girl with the book asked. We'll know it's here if we feel cold.

But no one did, not especially.

Later, when it was just her in the room, she wondered if they had done it right, and if they hadn't what would happen. Night after night she would sit in her room and look at the walls. Now I have you is what she would think.

Sometimes, though, she woke up in the middle of the night. She woke to the sounds the house made. Muttering, muttering, but also the whistle of a train. The sound of the train reminded her of the house by the sea. She would sit in her pale green room and think of the house by the sea and how the floor was covered with dirt and glass because her mother sat and stared at the fire even though it was the summer and for days at a time her father stayed at the water treatment plant where he did things he wouldn't talk about. Then she felt like the house, filled with sand and dust and cat hair and she would lick her lips. This was after the disappearance. After one day her brother just vanished and her mother wouldn't speak but wouldn't sleep either and went methodically about her business, cooking the same things over and over again, breakfast, lunch, and dinner, pancakes, peanut butter and jelly, and a burnt tuna noodle casserole, bitter and terrible to eat, and constantly rearranging the house, moving the furniture, cleaning the bureaus and the floors, but not too much, and even at times despoiling it, the house, even bringing in dirt, just the right amount, good, good, kneeling over the floor in the kitchen, kneeling there and rubbing the dirt into the off-white tiles, which were always cool against her cheek as she watched from under the kitchen table her mother, in a dirty blue robe and pale night gown, make the house, over and over, into the place it was the day before her brother went missing. Finally, one day her father put them both in the car and drove and drove until they reached a new house, a house with no memories, the house by the sea. At dusk you could lie in the dunes and watch the sun return to the ocean. You could put your ear to the ground and listen to unseen things moving, burrowing, beneath you.

Now, every afternoon it was the same. Now, every afternoon Tim and Marinella came over to Carol's house. What they did mostly was play games. They played Hide and Seek, Cops and Robbers, Hopscotch, Ghost in the Graveyard, Cave Explorer, Lost on a Hostile Planet, and Shadow People. They played each game methodically, exhausting its possibilities and then moving on.

The games weren't Tim and Marinella's first choice and in truth they weren't very good at them. Often Lucy had to shout corrections or even stop them in the middle of some confused gesture to offer reprimands and show them how a thing should be done.

Look, she told them. This is important. We're going to play until you get it right. If you can't do the simple stuff there's no way we can get to the next level.

This was in the backyard of Carol's house, on the small, wispy lawn, where she had once told them a story. Lucy sat on a wrought iron chair, her bony knees pulled up to her chest, a cigarette dangling on the edge of a cereal bowl and burning, burning.

But then the mother began to appear. First it was at Tim and Marinella's own house. Often, after Carol came back, the three of them would just go straight home and hang out there until the mother returned from work. At their own house Tim and Marinella wouldn't play any real games. Instead they watched TV or played video games and Lucy would watch them as they did. This is what she was doing when the mother first appeared. She was sitting on the couch while they played a game in which an angry pelican had to destroy, for some reason, an army of virulent, mutant mushrooms. She was watching the pelican chop up an angry-faced mushroom with an axe when she noticed the mother standing in the hallway opposite the carpeted front room where they were sitting. She was holding a tumbler filled with gin.

Lucy got up and walked over.

Sorry, she said. I didn't see you.

And you still don't, the mother said and wandered off into the kitchen.

Lucy followed her to the kitchen. The mother sat down at the table and stared dreamily at the wall and drank.

Is my shift over early? she asked.

Don't look for me, I'll get ahead, the mother sang tune-lessly. Then she put her head down on the table and her hair splayed out on its surface like the tentacles of some beached and dying sea creature. For a while the two of them just sat there.

After this, the mother was always at the house. She sat in various rooms and drank and didn't speak to anyone. Once Lucy found her sleeping fully clothed on the bed. She was in her dark blue business suit, on her back with a drink still in her hand, the glass tinkling and sweating. All over the carpet chicken bones were scattered. Everything else in the room was meticulously cleaned and placed. The bones seemed to have no origin and no purpose. The mother breathed in fits, loudly.

But soon enough she was also following them to Carol's house as well. She sat in the living room, the mother, and flipped through Carol's photo albums.

I don't think you can be here, Lucy said.

I can be anywhere, the mother said. Don't you know the rules?

The rules? she said

Understanding is not your kettle of fish, the mother said.

Tim and Marinella ignored their mother. They did so easily. It almost like they didn't see her at all. Instead they did the things they always did. They raced through the house and into the yard and through the house again and then went out back and climbed the tree. I can see you, they sang out to Lucy in unison.

What they needed was to get away. This is what Lucy decided. What they needed was new vistas and new experiences—she and Tim and Marinella—and to be as far away from the mother as possible. Mothers.

So one day she bundled them up and took them to the zoo. This, she felt, would be the first of many adventures. They would hit the road and cultivate disruption. She imagined them in a car racing through the craggy hills and mudflats of a vast desert (she had loved to read about deserts as a child) outrunning heat and sun and death. Together, she felt, they could be a map and a key; they could find a ladder and follow all the way down it to a glittering, impossible kingdom. Together they could transform.

The zoo seemed like a good enough place to start.

When she had first come here, to the city, Lucy sometimes visited the zoo. In truth, it wasn't a very good one. The animals lived mostly in cages or in big stone buildings calling themselves houses. They were lethargic and self-contained, the animals, sleeping mostly, or staring at vague points in the distance, primordial recollections of the pheromone-scented winds dimly firing, flickering in their lolling heads. But still people came. Even though it seemed to them the animals weren't very good at being animals, even though they didn't *do* anything, the people came and pointed and licked ice cream cones with their children.

Still she came. She came and watched them with absent-minded tenderness. The leopards, the antelope, the chimps, the komodo dragons. She liked their opaque eyes and their versatile mouths. Each animal a force, adapted to survive in uncaring lands. Like the komodo dragon, for example, capturing its prey with patience, waiting, waiting in the underbrush, long tongue flickering, flat head alert, claws tensed. There on its sunny rock in the zoo the dragon looked sleepy and pliable, something to be handled, caressed. But don't be fooled! It was ready, always ready. All the animals were. Ready to become, at any moment, their fearsome and majestic selves.

Why are we going to the *zoo?* Marinella asked with disdain.

They were riding in a cab.

Zoos are cool, said Lucy. They provide contact with a space of alienation and wonder and help us understand our place in the natural order of things

I think they're sad, Marinella said. All the animals are in cages and cages are terrible. And if they're not in cages they're one of those places where it doesn't seem like cages, where it's pretending like it's real, but it's still just cages, which is even worse.

Habitats, Lucy said, softly. They're called habitats. It means a place to live.

It means it's mean, said Marinella. To watch something be trapped and not even know it's trapped. I think that people who go to zoos are…, she thought for a moment. Sadistic, she said, finally. I think they're sadistic.

Where did you learn that word? Lucy said.

I have friends, Marinella said. Friends you don't even know about.

Once before Lucy had left, before she had packed a bag and slipped quietly out of the house one night, her father had taken her to the zoo. It was a different zoo, far from here, and it was hot and bright. They had watched the polar bears lie uncomfortably in the sun, their dirty fur and listless faces, and her father had said to her, his voice dull with sadness, at least we'll always have the zoo, and then put his arm gingerly around her shoulder and they stood there together.

Well, Lucy said, after a moment. That pretty well might be our place in the natural order of things.

The cab driver drummed his fingers on the wheel and hummed along to his blaring radio.

I want to see the anteater, said Tim. Its tongue is seven feet long and sticky and it eats up to ten thousand ants in a day. Ten thousand!

That's right, Lucy said uncertainly.

It's my favorite animal, Tim said. Except for the rhinoceros.

Marinella snorted. The rhinoceros? Could you *be* any more generic.

You know what Hemingway said about the rhinoceros? the cab driver piped up, raising his voice above the music. He said that shooting a rhino was the most disappointing experience he had in Africa. The African rhino is a dumb and willing target is what he said. Like picking up a Catalan prostitute.

The driver guffawed. Marinella laughed an eager laugh.

Tim looked perplexed. He stared at Marinella and then at Lucy, trying to decide between his options.

It's a joke, Lucy said to Tim. But not a very good one.

It's a great one, the cab driver said. Shows what you know.

The zoo was across the street from a funeral parlor called Worley and Sons and the cab dropped them there.

Lucy grabbed a wad of crumpled bills from an envelope and handed it to the driver, who held it like a used tissue.

Wow, he said. Thanks so much.

The funeral parlor had a bright turquoise front door and on it there was a sign that said: deposits in back. The street was quiet, empty. The neighborhood that contained the zoo did not look like a neighborhood that should contain a zoo. It was a long street with a shaded row of brownstones and a few darkened shops. It seemed like a place for gentle, finicky grandparents. But across the street the zoo's high, stone walls loomed.

There was also a sign on the zoo's entrance. That one said: Closed indefinitely. They all stood and stared.

Now what, said Marinella.

Lucy looked around. She grabbed the gate and rattled. She squeezed her arm into the space between the bars as far as it could go but it wouldn't go very far, just up to her bicep. She pulled it out and considered the gate.

We go up and over, she said, finally.

The gate wasn't very high and it wasn't particularly imposing either. There were no spikes and no wire. It wasn't electrified. It was just a gate. A simple obstacle necessitating only nimbleness and desire.

Lucy climbed over first.

Ok, she said. It's safe.

Tim and Marinella stood on the other side, warily.

Just climb over, she said.

They didn't move.

It's easy, she said.

They just stood there.

Ok, fine, Lucy said. Have fun waiting around. *I'm* going to the zoo.

She began to walk away.

No, Tim wailed, wait! I wanna go. Can we go, Mari, can we?

Marinella exhaled loudly.

Fine, she said with resignation.

She gave Tim a boost and began to follow him up. When Tim got to the top, he froze and looked with panic at the steep climb down

Don't stop, dummy, Marinella said.

A car drove by and slowed to a stop, idling just out of view.

Go! Marinella said. Go!

I can't, Tim whimpered. He straddled the gate, stuck between two of its thick wrought iron spires.

Hurry *up*! she yelled.

I *can't*, Tim yelled back at her and began to cry.

Lucy climbed back up near to him and held out one arm. The car reversed and came to a stop in front of the gate. A tan hatchback. Its driver wore a thick moustache and watched them with cool interest, taking drinks of something out of a white can.

Hold on to me and ease your other leg over, Lucy said to Tim. I've got you.

Tim sniffled and wiped his nose and slid into her arms, hanging tightly around her neck. His weight pulled at her, dragging them both groundward, and she had to grip the bars tightly, her hands stiff and sweaty, the socket of her arm aching, as they slid down, inch by inch.

Marinella quickly scrambled over the top and past them to the ground.

Come on, she said and darted into the zoo's winding parks.

Tim clung too tightly to Lucy's neck, panting.

I've got you, Lucy whispered to him. I've got you.

The driver made a gun out of his fingers and pointed and fired, smiling.

In the zoo a lot of the cages were empty. The tiger cage was empty and there was no hippo, no giraffe, and no zebras. Though they weren't entirely empty, the cages; they weren't impeccable. In most there was still straw and tufts of hair and bits of food and in some cases feces. It was like the animals had just been there, like they had vanished into thin air right before Lucy and the children arrived.

There's gonna be an anteater right? Tim asked Lucy, worriedly.

I'm sure it's still here, she said.

The anteater has big curved claws for digging into ant homes, he said. For *invading*.

Along the path a gaggle of peacocks pecked at the ground and called stridently to each other. In a landscaped patch of grass surrounded by a low gate, an animal that looked like big, angry guinea pig sat placidly and lounged in the sun, free of its cage.

Where *is* everything? Marinella asked.

Maybe they're cleaning, Lucy offered.

She looked around at the cages, the path, benches: all dirty, all in some state of early and gentle neglect

Or maybe they're going to change everything, she said. Reinvent it. Turn the zoo into place where the animals can live like they would in the wild, like real animals where they can run and climb and drink from streams and pools. Where they'd be safe.

Marinella looked at her appraisingly for a moment.

It would still be a zoo, she said, decisively. And it would still be freaky.

She ran ahead, eventually stopping in front of a cage some distance from them. Lucy and Tim joined her there. The cage said: *Vulpes zerda* The Fennec Fox. Inside a shiny, black bird with electric blue eyes hopped around gathering bits of ribbon, bottle caps, and shards of glass and placing them in specific spots around a small haphazard archway made of sticks and straw.

A display in front of the cage advertised FUN FACTS! It said: A male fox is called a Reynard! The female is called a Vixen! A baby is called a Kit! The fox's bushy tale helps the fox change direction quickly! It is sometimes called a sweep!

On the display there was also a red button to push so Tim pushed it.

A soothing but garbled voice began to speak to them about the fox. The fennec fox, the voice intoned, is a native of the Sahara desert located in present day Algeria. The Sahara is a forbidding place. Temperatures rise to 122 degrees Fahrenheit and have even exceeded 136 degrees! If you were caught in the Sahara desert there is no doubt you would die quickly and your death would be horrible, painful, and lonely. But this isn't the case for our friend the fennec fox! The fennec has several key adaptations to help it survive in such a terrible, hostile wasteland. Can you spot anything that would help the fox survive?

The bird in the cage where the fox should have been picked up a shard of glass and moved it from one side to the other. Once there it picked up a rubber band and carried it to where the shard of glass had been. Then it picked up a milk top and placed it in the center of its arrangement. Each of the objects were blue, and other objects too, piled in a corner of the cage, the exact same blue as the bird's considering eye. It hopped around the whole display for a moment as if contemplating its moves. It cocked its head and then began to call. The bird's call was surprising. It was pulsing and percussive and it sounded mechanical. It wasn't a song. It didn't carry the soul toward the elegant heavens. It was something else. A funnel of sparks, a burrow to a crystal cave. Something strange and magnetic. Lucy could feel it. She looked at Tim and Marinella. They could feel it too. The three of them, willing orphans waiting for the world's tender kiss, listening in a decrepit zoo, rapt and ready.

How the hell did you get in here? a voice behind them said.

Lucy stood and turned to see a young woman in khaki shorts and a matching button up khaki shirt. She stared at them with confusion and irritation. Lucy stared back.

The gate was open, she said, fumbling for the words.

We broke in! said Tim, gleefully.

Jesus Christ, Marinella sighed.

The woman considered them. She wore a tight ponytail and had a dark, etched face. She looked stern and beautiful in her sharp zoo uniform and under her critical gaze, Lucy felt childish and frivolous and she pulled nervously at the bottom of her baggy tank top.

Well, at least someone wants to see the zoo, the woman said. I guess. Though, your timing might've been better.

She sat down on the bench where they had just been so three of them sat back down too.

Still, the woman said, I suppose it's better than ghosts.

Ghosts? Tim said, eyes widened.

It's just a saying, Marinella said.

It is what you want it to be, the woman said.

In the cage the shiny bird had returned to its menagerie and was pushing its things around again.

That's not a fox, said Tim. A fox has a bushy tale sometimes called a sweep.

Really, the woman said.

The bird picked up a few pieces of straw and sticks from a pile near its little arch and placed them upon it, bolstering the structure.

It's a Satin Bowerbird, the woman explained after staring at it for a moment. Native to Queensland, Australia. The male of the species builds a complex structure out of sticks called a bower and then decorates it with anything blue it can find. It's a display behavior. It's meant to attract a mate.

They all looked at the bowerbird as it fussed over its display. Marinella peered at it closely, attentive. Lucy looked at the woman's hands, slender and strong, her shiny nails painted black, unchipped, ungnawed.

What's it doing here? she asked.

What is anything doing anywhere? the woman said and sighed. She smoothed out her shorts a little.

There's a crack in the aviary dome, she said, after a moment. All the birds have taken flight. The birds, the lions, the elephants. The tigers, the wombats, the ring-tailed lemurs. They're all over the city now or even farther.

The lions? Tim said.

Gone, the woman said staring at the bird. Gone, gone, gone. Off to other zoos and reserves and sanctuaries.

But not in the city, right? Tim asked.

No, honey, Lucy said.

People think zoo and they think crowds. They think zoo and they think children and yelling and the pounding sun and kiosk after kiosk of stupid merchandised animal crap. They think this, and then they think: I can watch this shit on TV. I can watch animals on high definition TV and have the same, no, a better experience. One without the heat and the smells and inconvenience of their terrible children. They think their eyes are the primary mode of knowing. The tyranny of the visual. But they've never fed a giraffe, have they? They've never felt its rough and reaching tongue. Or smelled the acrid musk of the clouded leopard as it marks its territory. You need to stand close to know. You need a zoo, the woman said. You'll see. Just the knowledge of a zoo, here in the beating heart of the city, just the thought of it, comforts; it stabilizes. Life will become grayer without the zoo. You'll see. The wild animal soul of the city. People don't know what they're about to lose.

Zoos are prisons, said Marinella.

Marinella, Lucy said.

You're a smart girl aren't you? the woman said. A clever girl.

Marinella smiled uncertainly.

Let me tell you something. Cleverness will only get you so far. You know what you experience when you stand close and know? You experience the bolt of understanding that we're still just animals. Look at this little guy. Displaying and building, waiting for a female to come and inspect his bower, to approve, to accept. It's why he does it: the parading, the calling, the showing off. Poor thing. Poor deluded thing. We've never even had a female bowerbird. Doesn't *that* sound familiar?

The woman smiled at Marinella.

Parading? Marinella said.

Parading, lifting, grunting, preening, smiles, smiles, smiles. The dance of seduction, the woman said.

It's just an instinct, Lucy said to Marinella. It's nothing special.

All instincts are special, the woman said.

Tim had been fidgeting during the whole conversation and finally got up and pushed the button again.

The fennec's defining feature is its giant ears, the voice told them. They may look cute to you, but the animal kingdom has no conception of cute. These ears help to keep them extra cool and to hear prey. The fennec is an omnivore. It has curved claws and sharp teeth. It can't wait to eat and will eat anything it can, including insects, lizards, snails, small rodents, birds, and eggs. This may sound disgusting, but that's what it takes to survive. What would you do to survive? Would you eat a bug?

No way, he said.

I keep bringing him stuff, the woman said, gesturing to the bowerbird. I bring more sticks and more hay. I bring the buttons and the glass. I seek them out. At first, it was kind of a caprice. I'd see something here or there and think suddenly I'll get that for the bowerbird. This was before the closure. Back when he had his own little enclosure. But then I found I couldn't stop. Every time I'd see something blue, I would get it. I would buy it or take it or shove it in my purse. My apartment is full of blue bottles, sheets of fabric, of ceramic vases just waiting to be torn or smashed and turned into fodder for his relentless courting. And after the zoo closed and the aviary fell apart...It's all I do know really. I'm beginning to feel like I'm his mate, like I'm the one he's building for. Or he's mine. It's him and me here. Me and him as the lights go out.

The call of the peacocks, insistent, shrill, and something else too, low and hollow, echoed through the zoo. The sun had gone behind flat clouds, casting everything in shade.

The woman walked them to the gate and let them out.

Don't think of this as an ending, she said. Think of it as a tragedy.

Outside of the funeral parlor two young men in black suits were smoking and readying themselves for entry.

You ever get tired of making them look so good? one said.

Nah, the other said. They wanna look that way.

That night Marinella called her. This wasn't necessarily unusual. At night sometimes Tim and Marinella would call. It was always late when they did. Too late.

Tell us a story, they'd say.

How did you get this number, she'd say.

One without brothers or sisters, they'd say.

Where is your mom? she'd say.

Wouldn't you like to know? they'd giggle.

But tonight it was only Marinella that called.

At first it didn't seem like anyone at all. The receiver breathed in echoing crackled waves.

Hello? she said. Hello?

Downstairs the girls were watching a movie. Recently they had decided to forgo the puppet shows in favor of films. They had a projector and a musical saw. They showed the films against the far wall of the circular room. The images, cast against the curving walls, stretched the characters into long and distorted apparitions. The musical saw accompanied them. Tonight, in these guises, men and women ambled through a rocky desert and conducted rituals in cavernous mountain retreats. They were often naked. Their bodies looked strangely soft. They were not her idea of bodies. The mouths opened and closed at odd intervals. Because there was no sound, you had to understand everything by facial expressions. But the expressions were hard to decipher.

I'm going to tell on you, Marinella said at last.

Lucy didn't say anything.

I'm going to tell mom about today and that you made us go and that you said you'd hurt us if we told.

Her voice was moist and insistent.

She'll believe me. You think she won't, but she will.

Lucy was sitting on her bed in her room. Her dark green room, which even though there was an empty room down the hall, was still her room, always her room. When she had first arrived at the house, one of the girls had led her upstairs and just left her there to stay. Often she could hear them talking, giggling, walking back and forth, the girls. But they never came upstairs. They never came to get her. Sometimes it felt like she was living in a brackish sea.

But during the day the whole house was empty. The girls were all at their jobs and sometimes she would sleep in the beds of the other girls. She wouldn't really sleep. Sleep was a trap. She would lie down on the bed and pretend to sleep. First she would put on the girl's clothes—her skirts, T-shirts, sweaters, even her underwear. Then she would brush her hair until it was shiny. And then she would lie on the bed and pretend she was sleeping. I am sleeping, she would think, her own clothes pooled in the center of the floor.

Tim, she started to say.

Tim will say what I say, Marinella said. His story is my story.

Lucy thought about Tim—Tim in his mask eating cookies, Tim holding her hand on the street, Tim running from small dogs and crying—and she knew that this was true. She knew what he was.

I want you to take me back to the house with the men, the Marinella said. I want you to take me inside.

Downstairs, among jagged rocks, elongated bodies writhed in red clay. In the sublime and desolate desert a man was being tormented by talking crows. The only sound was of the projector. It was a quiet hum. The man crawled slowly across the cracked desert floor. The crows hopped teasingly around him. They were saying something about desire. They were saying something about the insatiable. The man's face was the face of enervation.

The men, Marinella, Tim. Her brother, her parents, and life in the house by the sea. Some things were so fragile that to address them was to lose yourself in gestures.

Ok, she said.

Children can't be trusted, she thought.

Her mother said this to her once. It was at the house by the sea. The house by the sea was small and light blue. It was her house. This is how she thought of it. It was only for her. All around there were large dunes with spiky grasses. The house was nestled between them. Sometimes she wore red-checkered shorts. Sometimes she wore a loose white dress. Her mother didn't care. She sat on the front step and brushed her own hair. She pulled at its knots hard, but not too hard. Just enough so that she could feel it in her scalp. In front of her were two large dunes. She couldn't see the water, but she could hear it.

Her mother didn't care. She was too busy trying to remember things. Over and over again she wrote down what had happened the day of the disappearance. She did this in secret, hiding the evidence from her husband. If you don't tell him what I'm doing, her mother said, I won't tell him what you're doing. She didn't know what she'd been doing. When she was at the beach, she put her hands into tidal pools to watch them become like coral. When she was in the dunes, she dug up sand crabs and put them in a sealed jar. Were these the things? After the mother finished writing, she would read the account out loud. Every time she read the story it turned out slightly different. At first, it was little things: the placement of a chair at the kitchen table, the contentious appearance of a rectangle of sunlight on the living room floor, the sound of a barking dog. But the more she wrote, the more each version changed. Actions that had occurred in the morning began to occur in the afternoon. Clothing changed. Objects appeared and disappeared. The mother recognized this and at first it made her angry. As she read she would openly contradict her own account. No, she would shout angrily, No! That was *not* the color of his shirt! But then slowly she grew silent. She stopped reading the accounts aloud. Even her writing was silent. She wrote quickly but deliberately, and when she was done fed the papers directly to the fire. Her eyes were limpid and distant. It was summer. Still the fire was always going.

Children can't be trusted, her mother said. They were at the kitchen table. She and her mother. Her mother sat there in her dirty powder blue nightgown drinking coffee and looking out the window, which was small and a rectangle and had splotches and stains that no one cleaned. Occasionally she would turn her head and glance in her daughter's direction. For instance, I know you prefer your father, her mother said. But if I asked you point blank, if I said: Do you love your father more than me? I know what you would say. Without hesitation you would lie to me.

She sat at the table with her mother. She had been called there. The mother had found her out amongst the dunes and led her back here, to this table. The mother's face was a palimpsest of expressions. The father was a memory and a wish. She was sitting and listening. Sometime soon the father would walk in the door with a bag of donuts or maybe some bread. Once he had woken her in the middle of the night and led her into this very kitchen and sat her at this very table and pulled two store-bought, packaged cupcakes out of the refrigerator for them to share. Don't tell your mother, he had said. The cupcakes were cold and hard and sweeter than sweet. She had felt her feet on the cold, dirty floor. Soon he would return. But not soon enough. The light from the small window over the sink was bright but soft. She could smell the sea and its promises, its mysteries.

I tell you this, the mother said, quietly and firmly, not because I am angry but because I really believe you should endeavor to understand yourself a little bit better. She took a sip from her cup. The light from the window was pale like exposed skin. We all need to understand ourselves better, don't you think, sweetheart? We must all learn to comprehend our own essential cowardice. It's a worthy goal.

Years later when she left and went looking for her brother, when she visited hospitals and schools and woodland retreats, she remembered this conversation. Was the brother still a child? When did you stop being one? Occasionally she returned to the house and observed the movements there. She thought maybe he might have come to find them or that he too was watching. She imagined him among the tall grasses and weeds and sand also watching, watching her watching, and maybe taking notes.

Eventually, however, she stopped looking. She had taken her mother's jewelry and pawned it off piece by piece. The jewelry was all antique and expensive. Earrings, bracelets, bangles, pins. They had been her mother's mother's or her mother's mother's mother's. They had been handed down like a grudge. She sold the jewelry and searched and then sold it and lived. In hostels and cars and basement apartments she burned up her longing with hands and mouths, waiting for something to touch her on the shoulder, for someone else to love her and disappear.

The only thing she didn't sell was a gold pocket watch that no longer worked. It had been owned by their grandfather who had supposedly been sent to an institution after repeatedly attempting to set fire to his house while everyone was out. No one could say why he'd done it and he swore he'd never tell. Her brother had loved it.

The night she was supposed to take Marinella to see the men, the girls finally invited her to dinner. They sat at a long wooden table under dim swaying lights and passed food. Their faces looked sharp and expectant.

For an occasion of this order special plates were required. The plates were kept somewhere in the basement where no one ever went. A girl took her by the hand and led her there. The basement was cool and damp and soft, sagging boxes were scattered across the floor. There was a camera tripod facing a dirty brown couch against a wall. There was a dresser with drawers pulled out and clothes hanging out of them.

Together they knelt in front of a box. She and the girl. Lucy removed things one by one and placed them beside her. The girl shoved her hands in and pushed them around. She pulled out a photograph in a rusty metal frame. The photo was black and white and showed two women standing next to each other almost holding hands. They might have been twins but there was something off about them. They both had boyish haircuts and looked stern. The girl wordlessly showed the picture to Lucy, holding it delicately for a few moments, but then suddenly she tossed it aside and plunged her hands back in to the box.

After a few more minutes of silent searching, the girl began to tell her about how when she was thirteen she had tried to kill herself. She just started talking out of the blue. What she remembered, the girl said, is that she tried to hang herself from the ceiling fan in her parents' bedroom. It was afternoon and the room was dark. On the bed she had placed her stuffed animals and dolls to watch. She tested several times using a stepladder. She pulled up her legs to see if the fan would hold and then how long it would take before she began to lose consciousness. Finally, she jumped. Obviously she didn't die. Her mother found her in time, though it took a while to revive her. At least, this is what her mother told her when she talked about the incident, which is what her mother called it. The attempt. I was at the supermarket looking at cans of soup, she would say, and it suddenly occurred to me that had I made more often those chicken enchiladas you love so much and were always requesting I might have averted the incident. She also would leave little notes on the girl's pillow or on napkins in her school lunch. Thinking about you, the notes said, and the incident. In this way, the story slowly became her mother's. Soon she hardly recognized herself. You were always an unhappy child, her mother said. Morose and strange. You liked to pretend to die. In the pine tree behind the house, you'd imagine yourself attacked by poisonous spiders. She didn't remember the pine tree or spiders. Plus now she was having trouble with the suicide. Not the act. She could remember standing there, ready, looking at her dolls and animals, their unforgiving eyes. But what she couldn't remember is why. Maybe, she thought, she was playing a death game or maybe she really was unhappy, even though she didn't feel unhappy or remember feeling unhappy. One day she took all her clothes and books and stuffed animals and burned them in a bonfire in the backyard. Then she left. It wasn't until she ended up here that things began to make sense.

Wow, Lucy said.

Yeah, the girl said.

Mothers, she said.

Yeah, the girl said.

Should I get the plates? she asked.

They're already upstairs, the girl said.

At dinner all the girls placed forks delicately into their mouths at regular intervals. At the center of the table a grey freshwater fish with gelatinous eyes offered up its torn body. The girl who had taken her to the basement stood behind her and poured something into her cup. Inside of it the liquid looked black. Lucy could see, if barely, bits of her reflection there.

Will you drink the water? the girl asked.

Everyone looked at her.

After the dinner was over, Lucy went outside to smoke a cigarette. On the street in front of the house Marinella was already waiting. Tim was with her. Of course he was. They were standing on the sidewalk under a streetlight, which cast its orange light indiscriminately. Marinella was wearing a long, white dress, beaded across the chest and waist and webbed with lace about her neck. She had cut bangs into her hair, jagged and short. Tim was wearing a plastic cartoon cat mask. It was grey and striped and coyly smiling. Meow, he said, as she approached.

Lucy walked right past them without saying anything and they followed her, running to catch up. She led them through the neighborhood once again. They turned and turned and turned. The house was not hidden; it was not hard to find. There was no secret password, no mystical incantation to make it appear. It didn't look haunted. It was just a house in the neighborhood, a place where certain kinds of men lived. Still she knew all too well why Marinella wanted to find it.

She counted the lights in the windows as they walked. Lights of yellow, orange, red. And thought about the people who lived inside those windows, who lived there and didn't look out. Normal, ordinary lives. A husband washing wine glasses by hand. He says something to his wife. She laughs. Or no, does she say something back? Something tart? Then they all watch television: a man, a woman, a boy, a girl. The light in the window flickers and assembled there in the aura of the television the family experiences the anesthesia of togetherness, their shared dream reflecting back at them. But here she was walking with a cat and a virginal bride, walking towards something that was bound to be cataclysmic one way or another.

Finally they arrived. She stopped in front of the house and Marinella looked it over.

This is it? Marinella said.

Yes, she said.

Are you sure? Marinella said.

I'm sure, she said.

It looks different, Marinella said.

Meow, Tim said.

It looks like a house, she said, because that's what it is. It's a house. It's just a house.

It looks...plainer, Marinella said.

Sometimes the house you want is not the house you get, she said.

Meow, Tim said again.

Marinella kicked at the sidewalk for a bit and looked at the house. She squatted down on the ground and peered up at it. She considered. Ok, she said.

The house—gigantic, ornate, dilapidated—seemed as if was buckling under an unseen weight. It had a long, rectangular wooden porch accessible only on one side. They walked up the steps, which were weathered and kind of spongy and creaked under their collective weight. They came to the door and knocked and waited.

What do we do now? Marinella asked.

It's your adventure, Lucy said.

Marinella knocked again. She looked around helplessly. She was just a girl. She had incoherent longings and fears.

Why don't you open it? Tim said.

Marinella gave her brother a look. And then she did.

The hall of the house was wider than it was long. It wasn't quite a square but it wasn't a proper rectangle either. It felt both spacious and cramped. The floor was a tessellation of dirty black and red tiles. At the very end of the hall a magnificent, rickety wooden staircase presided. The whole place was quiet, still. The house did not look like a patients' residence, that was for sure. It looked like more like a decrepit mansion, a decrepit mansion where the only surviving member of a once powerful family lived, surrounded by her porcelain dolls, nurturing grievances and desires. Lucy expected an old, delusional woman to come down the stairs at any moment.

Tag, yelled Tim suddenly. You're it!

Both Tim and Marinella immediately ran from her, giggling. Tim up the central staircase; Marinella into the dark archway to the left of the staircase.

No! Lucy called after them. Jesus! This isn't the time!

Upstairs she could hear Tim giggling and skittering, the sounds quieting, receding into the unknown. The archway on the other hand was completely silent.

Marinella? she called out into the dark.

Nothing.

Marinella. I'm coming back, don't move.

She climbed the staircase to the second floor. It was a wide hallway with three rooms on each side, the doors all closed. At the end of the hall was a bay window filled with dusty large, square pillows.

Tim? she coaxed. Tim? She could hear him again; his muffled voice burbled through the walls.

Lucy followed the sound to a room and entered it. Now she could hear him clearly. There was no one in the room but she could hear him clearly. His voice was coming from a back room, the door of which was slightly ajar. In this back room Tim was sitting on the floor and talking to a young man, who was sitting on an unmade bed.

Tim, she said sternly.

But sometimes I keep it in my shoes, Tim was saying to the young man. Because nobody thinks to check there.

Tim, she said again.

I'm not Tim, said Tim. I'm The Cat.

The Cat, said the young man, has been telling me all about my own magical qualities. He smiled a quick, tired smile.

He doesn't know! said The Cat.

Sometimes, the young man said, it can hard to get a grip on things like that.

Tim, she said. It's time to go. We have to find your sister.

Is it, said the young man. Is it really? He exhaled smoke. That's a shame. I'd think The Cat would know when it's time for him to go. They seem to be in tune with those kind of clocks, cats do. What do you think, Cat?

The Cat says not yet, said The Cat.

The room was small and the color of curdled cream. In it there was just the twin bed and small white dresser. The sheets on the bed looked like they hadn't been washed in some time. They appeared despoiled.

Besides, the young man said, sisters aren't so easily found. Sometimes you think you've got one but it turns out you're actually holding a fish.

A fish! The Cat giggled.

Or a bird, the young man said.

Please, Lucy said, you're not helping.

That depends on where you're standing, he said. In your case, the doorway. In my case.

He shrugged and looked around.

The young man tossed a package of cookies to Tim, who took several and tossed the package back. They were not the sandwich kind. They were round and cream-colored and looked dry. Tim slipped his mask up slightly and took a bite of cookie and chewed quickly. For some reason this gesture disgusted her a little. This slipping off of one expression to reveal the underface. She watched him helplessly, this creature of two mouths, the one that consumed and the other that commented. When he was finished chewing, the mask came back down again. She shivered.

Feel better? the young man asked.

The Cat nodded.

And you? What about you? Do *you* feel better?

Lucy didn't know what he meant. But still she nodded, too.

Why don't you come in? he said. You're making us all nervous.

But she didn't want to come in. To enter this communion, to sup from their current, it seemed terrible to her.

You know what a doorway resembles? the young man asked.

A rhinoceros, Tim said excitedly.

No, he said. No. Not that.

For a moment he seemed troubled. He closed his eyes and mouthed some words.

A hippopotamus, Tim said and bounced a little while he said it.

No, he said. But it's right there, it's…it's…

A hummingbird, Tim shouted out and fell into a fit of giggles.

Goddamn it! the young man shouted, pounding the bed with his fist and upsetting the carton of cookies.

Briefly the Cat turned back into Tim. Inside his mask, Tim's eyes grew wide.

It's gone, he said, quietly, returning to his former torpor. But not totally gone. It's outline is still there.

He licked his lips.

Words, you know?

Tim, Lucy said. The Cat, she corrected herself. We need to go. We really, really need to go.

No, Tim said impertinently. I don't *want* to.

Lucy strode suddenly, quickly forward and grabbed him forcefully by the arm. That's enough, she said. She began to yank him out of the room. She pulled at his arm, but he recoiled instantly. No! he screamed. No! His scream was inhuman, something vestigial and reptilian, and as he screamed, he struggled against her grip, flailing and kicking, kicking and flailing, right in the shins and knees, over and over, his screaming and kicking, until she let go, she just let go, and he dropped to the floor, scooting under the bed, where he stayed sobbing quietly. She slunk down right in the spot where Tim himself had just been sitting.

The young man remained unmoved. He chewed his cookies.

Wow, he said after a few minutes. You're really not good at this, are you? I mean, I think you thought you were good, but in the end, you just couldn't ask for a worse result.

The sound of Tim snuffling was quiet but persistent.

I, Lucy said. I don't, she began.

The young man's eyes were green and wide and bright.

I was being reasonable, she said, finally.

Everyone always is, the young man said. But if you say it real fast over and over again, then what have you got?

He smiled again.

Lucy felt dizzy from the smoke, yes the smoke certainly, but also the light and the room and the young man whose voice kept circling and circling. She was more than a little tired. And Marinella was somewhere downstairs. A girl downstairs. A girl alone: who knew what she was encountering?

Results are what matter, said the young man. They'll tell you differently. They'll tell you that effort matters, or that the process matters, and that what's important is registering the minute vibrations every day. Did you know that this is how bats comprehend the world? And cockroaches and scorpions? The crawling things. The lowest orders. Through tiny hairs or antennae. That's their modus. They *feel* these things, these minute things, they *feel* them all over and move one way or another based on nothing more. Can you even imagine that? A whole world of feeling? A universe ordered through sensation? Many people just call that hell. Of course many people believe quite seriously that their nerves extend invisibly outward in all directions. Auras, energy fields, ghostly souls. Once a man believed his nerves extended to Heaven itself, which I find a bit problematic. The direction of Heaven being an open question, right? Is it at the edge of the universe? Is it somehow *between* the universe? All that dark matter no one knows what to do with? He believed that he could save himself and the world from God's maniacal injunctions or something by becoming a woman. The man in question did. This seems more plausible to me. Plausible like a hat is plausible. You know. You have to confuse God. That way he won't know exactly what to say to you. He won't brand you with His words, His terrible words, know what I mean?

Again she nodded under his gaze.

I'm boring you, he said, matter-of-factly. I don't mean to bore you. There nothing worse. Hey, The Cat, he called down to Tim. Maybe you want to come out? Come out and play with the big kids?

Maybe, Tim sniffed.

Maybe is for Mondays, the young man said.

He stood up and stretched and surveyed the room from his new position. He was wearing white flannel pajama pants with steaming coffee cups all over them. He raised his arm over his head and pressed his palms against the ceiling.

Has anyone ever adequately described your beauty? the young man said to Lucy.

He began to bounce on the bed as he spoke. He kept his hands pressed against the ceiling.

I suspect not, he said. It was my parents' belief that one's beauty should always be described. Precise words for every occasion. A foundation for sensible living.

Lucy could hear Tim scuttling underneath the bed.

Stop it, she said.

My mother's mother considered her daughter to be plain. Or at least this is the view my mother took based solely on her own mother's silence regarding physical beauty.

Please, she said.

It's a little confusing, the young man said. I understand. But what I'm trying to express is the inadequacy of this kind of thinking. The inherent problems of establishing a merely reactive systems of values. Although to be fair, I'm not sure my mother was ever what you would call, you know, conventionally beautiful.

Stop it! Lucy yelled at him. You're gonna hurt him!

The young man stopped and looked at her. The mattress continued to bounce a little and he with it.

I thought you *wanted* him out, the young man said.

I did, she said. But…

This is exactly my point, the young man cut her off. Certain decisions, he said, require a choice between pain and different pain.

Tim, she said, softly. It's ok. Come on out. It's, it's gonna be ok.

Yeah, the young man said. Arise from your splendid sepulchre. Everything's going to be just fine.

Meanwhile, Marinella was watching a man painting a bad mural on a dingy wall. She was in the basement. The man was painting a pastoral scene. In it many children were playing in a forest. The forest was neither dark nor dense. In fact it was quite pleasant. The grass was green, the trees were green, the sun was yellow. The sun did not have a face but you could tell it was smiling. It was the sun's color that gave it this impression.

The children, on the other hand, did have faces. But their faces didn't say anything. They looked serious but not glum. They looked like children. Their mouths were shaped in little lines and sometimes Os and they were playing. They played in groups of twos and fours. Sometimes they looked like they were jumping; sometimes it looked like they were sleeping. But they certainly were not sleeping. Their eyes were open and they stared at each other and the forest.

These children weren't alone. There were also animals in the forest and the forest animals also played. But they didn't look happy to do so. Their eyes were red and their teeth were pointy and bared. The children, however, did not seem to notice them.

There was something disorienting about the mural. Maybe it was the sun or maybe it was the animals or maybe it was the children and their faces and the fact that they all looked exactly alike. But maybe it was because the children's heads weren't shaped like heads at all. Maybe it was because instead they were shaped like houses. Little squares with triangles on top. Little children with houses for heads.

When Lucy and Tim and the young man found Marinella, the painter was affixing hair to the children's heads with glue. He cut a little from his own head and then glued it onto the little house-shaped heads of the children.

Marinella, Lucy called out to the girl. Honey, she said.

Marinella turned and looked at them, then she turned back to the mural.

Hey! the young man said, You've found Patrick! Hi Patrick.

Shhh, said Patrick.

What's he doing? Marinella asked.

He's painting, the young man said. Obviously.

I mean with the hair.

Still painting, I imagine.

Shhh, Patrick said again.

Patrick, the young man said with mock grandeur, is expressing himself. He is exploring the perils of his very own interior landscapes and living to tell about it. Or at least that's what he thinks he's doing. Isn't that right Patrick?

Please, Patrick said.

The young man walked over to Patrick and put his arms around Patrick's shoulders. Patrick winced. He hunched his shoulders up and looked around the room with pleading agitation. Together they looked at Patrick's work.

But if you ask me, I mean, how can you really consider this self-expression. Children? A forest? I mean, Jesus, right? It's so…obvious. Why not just paint a frowny face and write, Mommy doesn't love me, in big erratic letters. Is this really delving deeply into your episode? Is this honestly the best you can do? These are the questions I ask him. Don't I Patrick?

The young man tightened his grip around Patrick's shoulder. Patrick's eyes were red and filmy.

It's entirely possible that the answers to these questions are yes. Unlikely, sure. But possible? Why not? People are a lot less singular than they like to think. One day my sister came home from school and sat down at the kitchen table and told me that her life was over. She was dramatic, my sister, that's for sure. In this case, though, I don't think she was exaggerating. She said, Today I realized I'm not special. What a terrible realization, right? The sudden death of magic. It's like finding out there is no Santa Claus.

The young man stopped short.

Sorry, Cat, he said to Tim.

He already knows, Marinella said. I told him as soon as I found out.

The young man released his grip on Patrick, who turned around and stared at his wall.

You're a piston, he said admiringly to Marinella. You're a key.

Tim pressed up against Lucy's leg and hugged her with his free arm. He had been holding her hand since they left the bedroom, holding and squeezing and waiting for reciprocation. His other hand was injured. It was red and purple and swollen and he had been kind of cradling it against his stomach. Something had happened when he was under the bed, when he was hiding from her, when he had made his decision. Now he wrapped that wounded hand around her legs.

My parents left a gift under the tree and its box in the basement, Marinella explained. Why would Santa leave the box? It was ice skates. It was a dumb gift anyway.

You're a lightning bolt, the young man said. You're a stroke.

Tim whispered something to her.

Marinella looked at the young man and then looked at Patrick.

Parents do their best, the young man said. But they lack flexibility. Not to mention all the right hands. Anyway, it's the awareness that counts.

Where's everyone else? Marinella asked.

Everyone? the young man said.

I saw you once, Marinella said. I saw you but it wasn't just you. There were more. There was a whole bunch of you.

Oh, the young man said. Right. There used to be. But they left.

Left?

Departed, the young man said. Yes.

That's not true, Marinella said.

Truth, the young man said. It's never just an apple.

Tell me where they are, Marinella said, her voice rising, quavering.

Tim whispered to her again and tugged on her hand.

People are always leaving, the young man said. They are always fro-ing and to-ing. They think it will make them real again. Or less real? One of the two anyway.

I want to go, Tim whispered to her.

That's not true, Marinella said, raising her voice.

People think of this as a refuge but it's not a refuge, he said.

There have to be more, Marinella said.

Lucy wriggled her hand out of Tim's grip and walked over to Marinella.

Because I *saw* them, Marinella began to cry. I *saw* them.

There is no refuge, the young man said. There is no home.

She put her hand on Marinella's shoulder and Marinella let it rest there.

There are only systems after systems after systems, the young man said.

I saw them, Marinella said, now softer. They were in the sun and they...did things and they were happy. They were together and they were happy.

Once I wanted what you wanted, the young man said. I was benighted as a mole in the ground. *I can be dissolved* is what I thought. But nothing is what you think it is. Nothing is ever what you think it is. It will always be what it is *because* you think it. You're the common denominator.

Don't listen to him, Lucy said to Marinella.

They were happy, Marinella said, softly. They had a place to be.

You know what? said the young man. There never was anyone else. It was always only me and Patrick. Isn't that right, Patrick? the young man said and patted Patrick on the back.

Patrick jumped under the touch and turned abruptly and hit the young man right in the mouth. The young man reeled back and then doubled over. He spit. It was a mixture of saliva and blood and it hung from his mouth in a long strand. For a moment he looked like he was going to charge at Patrick. His eyes gleamed with intention. He looked feral. But then he turned his head and smiled.

Can we go now? she asked Marinella.

Marinella sniffed and looked at her.

Wow, Patrick, the young man said, licking his lips. Now we're getting somewhere.

The next day Lucy arrived at Popsicle's house as usual, ready to work. She was going to refocus, she told herself. No more children, no more schemes. She had a vocation right here, a fire worth tending. When she'd brought Tim and Marinella home to sneak in the way they had snuck out, they stood in front of the house together for while not knowing what to do. They were silent and the house was silent and the dark, purplish sky was clouded making what stars there were difficult to see. Marinella seemed to understand now what would happen. She seemed to understand how sometimes adventures stop rather than end. How people try and fail but attempts don't necessarily constitute currency. She stood away from Lucy. She was a girl but she was the first-born. She knew all about leaving. Tim, however, still clung to her. He had taken off his mask and was holding it in his good hand. His eyes were liquid with tears. She took his bruised hand and kissed it and then gave it to Marinella to hold and a said, Listen guys: I have to go on vacation for a while. With my family. I'm not sure when I'll be back but I will be back. I promise. I'll bring you something. Souvenirs. Then she left.

Carol opened the door in her usual way—slowly, peaking out first and then opening it wide—but today she wouldn't let Lucy in. She stood there in her doorway blocking the entrance. She wasn't pushy but, in her own gentle way, she stood her ground.

I've been talking with some friends, Carol said. And they think that things here have gone too far. I'm a good person, the woman said. A nice person. A person who, when push comes to shove, believes in things. I trust. I'm trusting. I'm not bragging. I don't mean to boast. It's just a fact. And I've always regarded this fact with a little bit of awe. As if life itself handed me a precious little box. So I've been talking with my friends. And my friends think, and I agree, that you have been taking advantage of this fact. This gift. My precious little box.

I know I haven't been around as much, Lucy started.

Too much! Carol exclaimed. You've been around too much.

She was clearly agitated.

Lucy didn't know what to say. Carol stood there trembling slightly. Beyond Carol's agitated body, Lucy could see the dim and familiar room with all its pictures and covered chairs.

I just want to help, she said. To help you with your problem.

My problem! Carol exclaimed. My problem! My problem is that you are endeavoring to steal my Popsicle! Steal him right out from under me! With each trick you teach and every treat you give, I see you are slowly laying claim.

Carol was now shaking and she grasped the doorjamb for comfort and support.

And that, the woman said firmly, I cannot allow.

Then she slammed the door, leaving Lucy standing there, bewildered on the doorstep, the day suddenly shapeless and threatening.

Lucy sat down on the stoop. It felt colder than it looked like it should feel. A car rolled slowly by blaring a jumble of sound and a gap-toothed, giddy tow-headed girl who had been waving indiscriminately at the world just before stopped for a moment to stick out her tongue directly at Lucy.

This couldn't be the end, she thought. She had better stories for Popsicle. Wonderful stories. In ancient Greece sick people used to be licked into health by sacred dogs. In other times people carried dogs around to ward off madness. Popsicle was capable of so much.

That night she looked at the website for the first time in a long time. She scrolled through the posts. There was a section on the website where people could gather to lament their lost animals. Here the posters lovingly described their animals' own precious and particular behaviors; they told long, desperate stories about their terrible circumstances; they offered affectionate tributes to painfully brief lives and their own heroic love. They were determined, composed—assembled daily in the soft shapes of their own mourning. Lucy clicked on one after another. Recently a woman had been writing eulogies about her cat who had died several years ago. Every time someone else posted about the death of *their* pet this woman responded with the story of her cat. Just that evening someone had written about the tragic death of his golden retriever, Zippy, who had come to his demise naturally, after a protracted and incremental failing of organs and parts. Our animals keep our memories, the woman posted in reply. Every day I feel myself moving away from the self I have been towards something dark and diffuse. But I am certain that my friend is waiting for me on the other side. I am certain he is waiting there, holding with him all my life's days.

Part 2

When she was still a girl, and before the disappearance, she and her brother would play dead bodies. Dead bodies meant lying next to each other, silent and immobile, in their parents' bed. Almost touching, but not touching. It was always afternoon when they did this and their parents' bedroom was dim and empty. When you are dead, her brother said, it's dark, but not too dark. At first they still wore clothes, but slowly they took them off until they were naked. Degrees of death, her brother said. The desire to touch him consumed her. Like there was an animal under his skin that needed petting. But touching was forbidden. What do you think about when you're dead? she asked. Death means not thinking, he said. But sometimes ants and worms come to eat. And yesterday a crow pecked out my eyes. Much to her awe he could be dead for hours. But all she could think was the word "dead." Dead, dead, dead, she thought, in hopes of making it work.

The problem was looking. Even though it was against the rules, she stole glances. This looking was a kind of touch. He would lie on his back in the middle of his bed, his eyes wide open, his lips bright. In the dim light, his body was pale and delicate. She hoped that she was as beautiful dead as he was. He was perfect. Later she would lock herself in her room and remember him. In the memory he had no genitals. His arms were crossed gently upon his chest. His skin was the color of white dinner plates. Behind the memory was her hand, hovering and waiting for its chance.

But there was also this: she had a photo of the beach where her brother disappeared. In it she and her brother stand in front of their parents. They wear multicolor swimsuits and determined smiles. Behind them the ocean looks grey. The photograph was taken by a passer-by. He was a pudgy, sunburned man in a floppy hat and large sunglasses. What did this have to do with her brother? She remembered her mother running around kitchen table and throwing things. Things in this case meant dinner plates, pots, glasses. The floor was covered with shards and dust. But this was this only thing she could remember. If she had a picture of the beach without the family, or at least without her brother, she thought she might remember differently. She might remember what her father did. She might remember where her brother went. Although she did remember that she had been collecting small rocks, which she later kept in a jar in the back of her closet. Occasionally talked to them as if they were her brother.

He came back four months later, but it was not really him. He told her parents that someone had taken him and told him religious truths and that he had, for a time, believed them. This explanation satisfied her parents, but parents are easily satisfied. They merely wanted to look at him. Just look at you, they said. Let's take a picture. When she held the two pictures next to each other, the difference was obvious. Something about the hair and the eyes and the mouth. At night she would sneak into his room to watch him sleep. His body splayed differently. The way someone dies is like a fingerprint or a snowflake. Who are you? she whispered to him while he slept.

Some things were the same, though. For example they still played games. Once, they were playing in the warm, crepuscular light, near the woods. It was a new game and the rules were complicated. First, she told him, I'm lost. I'm lost in another world, which is right here but we can't see it. So I'll go over there and pretend I can't see you but I'll be looking for you the whole time. Because I'm lost, she said. Ok, he said. But you have to be looking for me too. It's the only way I can get out, if you're looking for me. But once you find me you have to prove to the creatures that you are worthy of me. You have to do a dance. It has to be convincing but also entertaining. She looked at him. He stood there, his hands jammed into his pockets. He was looking at the ground. Maybe you should just run in place a lot, she said. Ok, he said. She walked some distance away from him and in preparation rubbed some dirt on her face and into her hair. Then she concentrated on being lost. She began to spin with her eyes closed and after that she crawled around on the ground and after that she got up and staggered left and right and waved her arms searchingly in the air crying out for him. Help me, she cried. I love you, she cried. But he didn't attend her cries.

Even though he was supposed to cry out for her, he didn't cry out. In fact he wasn't even looking at her. Instead he stood at the threshold to the woods, peering into them. You're not doing it right, she yelled at him. She ran up to him and stood beside him but he didn't seem to notice her. He looked into the woods or at them or into and beyond them. His pale skin was unusually cold. You're not doing it right, she said softly. It was getting close to dusk. The light had stopped looking warm. She looked down and noticed that his feet were bare. His toes curled into the dead grass. Where were his shoes?

She decided to make a list. She wrote the following things.

He smells different.

He does not look at Mom when she talks.

He looks at other things for too long.

His fingernails are always dirty.

Things = walls, the woods, squirrels, his hands.

He smells sharp.

She wrote these things in a green notebook with a happy orange cat on it. At first she kept it under her pillow, then she kept it in her sock drawer. Then she decided to move it every day. She woke up early and found the new place and hid it. Then she wrote the name of the location on a scrap of paper and swallowed it. When she wrote, she said the name of the place over and over to herself. When she ate the paper, she closed her eyes.

At night she could hear him wandering the house. His feet were light against floor, almost like he was barely touching at all.

The house was filled with doors and mirrors. The mother was always installing a door or hanging a mirror. Often she put them in places where neither needed to be. There were doors for every entrance and every exit to every room and at least one mirror on each wall. A door between the parlor and the dining room, between the dining room and the kitchen, a door blocking the entryway from the rest of front hall. Everything that could be enclosed would, must. She kept changing the door to the brother's room, almost weekly it seemed, no door was just right. Until one day she brought one home and installed it and that became the brother's door forever. It had four detailed panels depicting in relief the capture and death of some animal that looked like a dog but wasn't a dog. It had an opaque blue glass knob.

Safe in her own room, behind her own closed door, in the darkness, she could hear the sounds of his passage coming closer or moving farther and farther away, the slow creaking of hinges, the deliberate click of the latch, becoming almost unrecognizable, just one more whisper in the ever murmuring house. I am awake, she would think without sitting up or even opening her eyes. I am awake.

She wrote:

He killed a bird. I watched him do it. The bird was soft
and tiny. It was not brand new but it was not old. It was
in between. He did it with his hands. The bird would not
stop chirping. Something was wrong with it. It was in the
tall grass. It was nestled there. He scooped it up. I could
not see what was wrong with it. He scooped and kissed
it. Its chirping was terrible. He closed his hands around
it and squeezed. He squeezed it slowly. He was gentle.

Then one night he crawled in bed with her. He was there when she woke, his eyes on her. His strange and opaque eyes. You're cold, he said. She didn't say anything. I had a bad dream, he said. Oh, she said. He put his arm around her and they stayed like that for a little while. Then he said, I was following this dog into the woods. It was one of those small dogs with really large heads. The kind that looks like an old man. A man that got so old he became a dog. This dog had escaped the house, he said, and it was his responsibility to bring it back. If he didn't there would be consequences, undefined yet dire. For the dog was a responsibility. It was something terrible bequeathed to them, something they had to satisfy. So they kept it in the cellar and fed it odd bits of meat and didn't call it anything at all. But the woods was a different story. In the woods it was docile. He said: when I lagged behind it would wait for me to catch up. I began to feel that it had something in store for me. Like it was going to tell me something and it became clear to me that what it was going tell me was something important, something about the house and its captivity. I kept walking. Eventually I found it in a grove. An elegant grove. An elegant grove? she said.

It lay there. Its head raised toward the sun. Its eyes closed. I reached down to pet it because I knew that when I did it would begin to speak. It would tell me what I needed to know. But when I reached down to pet it instead I found myself sticking my hand in the knothole of a log. That's when I woke up. He gave her a knowing look. That's it? she said. Yeah, he said. For a little while longer they lay there. His arm felt heavy on her chest. His breathing was deep and she thought he was asleep. But then suddenly, he said, when I woke up I remembered playing near the woods once when we were on vacation. Where we saw grown-ups moving slowly through the trees, dressed like they were going to church. Remember? he said. Yes, she said, though she didn't remember this at all.

But there was also another girl and it was the girl who said it. She was tall and thin with wispy hair and large eyes. She liked green popsicles and let the juice drip on to her hand without cleaning them. They didn't know where she came from. One day she just appeared.

They were in the backyard. They weren't really playing, but they weren't separate either. She was digging up plants, pulling them right out of the ground, roots and all. She liked how at first it was hard and then suddenly it was easy. She liked the feeling of tearing free. Sometimes, she imagined she was the plant and it satisfied her. The brother didn't look at her when she did this. He was busy doing things brothers did.

The girl stood at the edge of the grass and watched them.

Are you new? the brother asked.

No, she said.

Do you want to play? the brother asked.

I don't know, she said.

The brother shrugged. The girl continued to stare. The dirt from the plant's roots fell lightly onto her arm. She carefully rubbed it into her skin.

Later she and the girl were friends. It happened like this:

She was in her room, playing with her dolls. It wasn't going very well. There were too many of them and it was hard to tell what they wanted from her. She pushed them around desultorily. The girl was at the door. How long had she been there? She didn't cross the threshold. For a while all she did was stare. You're doing it wrong, the girl said finally. She didn't say anything. You need at least one more to play "End of the World," the girl said. This shocked her. She didn't think she was playing anything. She looked around. Here, the girl said and entered the room. She arranged the dolls on the bed and they sat on the floor. They stared at the dolls and the dolls stared at them. Now we're ready, the girl said. See?

The mother thought the girl was a school friend and they let her believe it. My goodness, the mother said, just look at you! She took an orange dishrag to the girl's face and wiped it brusquely. There, the mother said, satisfied.

When the girl stayed overnight, they would tell stories about melancholy ghosts and watch the brother in secret. This was not an easy thing to do. The brother was sullen and clandestine. Usually he hung out in the basement. In the basement it was cool and damp and there were stacks of old books and too many chairs and shelves with porcelain animals and clocks that did not work. She didn't like it. It smelled musty. It was under the ground. Who likes to be under the ground? Crawling things, that's who. But when the girl was there they went down anyway. They snuck down the staircase on their hands and knees, whispering admonitions to each other as they went. The girl always went first. They always peered around the corner to see.

One night, they saw him talking to himself. He stood in different places and said things in different voices. Sometimes he was agitated, sometimes he was calm. At one point it seemed like he was choking. He grabbed his own throat and his eyes got big and he sank to his knees. His eyes were closed. He slumped to the ground. He was going to be dead, she thought excitedly. Dead, dead, dead. But he didn't stay there at all. He got up and then did other things, spoke in other voices. She didn't really see him do these other things. She just stared at the spot where he had lain.

Does he always do that? the girl asked, after they had crawled back upstairs. They were in the kitchen, eating cereal out of big bowls.

What? she said.

Talk to himself like that.

I don't know.

Why not?

He does different things, she said.

Like what? the girl said.

I don't know, she said and put a spoon in her mouth. He's always doing something, she said after she swallowed.

The girl glared at her a little. Clearly she was unhappy with the answer. For a while they scraped their big bowls in silence.

He didn't used to, she said, quietly. I don't think he did. I can't remember. Maybe he did.

The girl looked at her thoughtfully. Do you feed them? she asked, finally.

She looked at the girl.

Your memories? the girl said. Do you feed them?

She wanted to say yes, but she didn't know what it would mean if she did.

Here, the girl said. She took her by the hand and they went into the mother's room. For a little while the girl looked in some of the porcelain dishes that waited on the mother's darkly burnished bureau. The dishes had tops that resembled the heads of different, delicate flowers. She opened them one by one. She reached into one and fished around. Its top was a swirling pink rose. Here, she said, pulling out a single needle and holding it between her fingers.

Give me your hand, the girl demanded.

She hesitated.

It's important, the girl said.

She gave the girl her hand. The girl held it gently, caressing it with her thumb and forefinger. See? she said. Then she quickly stabbed the pad of her index finger with the pin.

Ow, she cried out.

Shhh, the girl said and then squeezed the finger hard. Shhh. A small dollop of blood emerged from the pinprick. A red pearl.

You have to feed them, the girl said. If you want them to come. You have to feed them.

After that, she and the girl always played the game they called feeding. They did this under an overgrown lilac bush near an alley in the backyard. They crawled underneath it one at a time. They crawled on their bellies. The small branches scratched at their backs as they went.

Inside the bush everything was different. It was quiet and close. They sat across from each other, Indian-style. She held out her hand in front of her and the girl grabbed it. Her arm was straight. Her palm faced up. Is there anyone here who wants to have memories? the girl would intone. I'm the one who wants them, she would say. Then the girl would stab her finger with the needle and squeeze. It was deeper than the first time in the kitchen. The blood fell in slow drops onto the dirt. As it fell she would say things out loud. Once, when I was little, I almost died, she said. My brother and I were on a mountain and I wasn't looking and almost walked off the mountain. But my brother saved me. He pulled me back at the last minute. The girl didn't ask any questions; she just listened. The stories came out. The blood mixed with the dirt. Her finger ached. The girl stared straight ahead.

Afterwards they would write down the stories in a little notebook. It was the same one where she wrote things about the brother. Sometimes it was hard to tell what was true and what was memories. Inside the lilac bush there was a holy silence. Outside she carried the needle in a pocket of her dress. Don't look, she'd always say to the girl when it was time to pull the needle out.

Meanwhile, in the living room, the brother sat with impunity in an antique chair. The mother knelt beside him and rested her head upon his lap. Her eyes closed.

The room was dark in the way it was always dark—shadowy, cavernous, unpronounced. Inside, objects were waiting. When she was little, she would stand at the threshold of the room and peer into it. Her brother told her that inside the room was a witch and if you stopped long enough in the center of the room the witch would appear and spirit you away to her nest underneath a lake to feed your fingers, one by one, to her hatchlings. But she could only take you if you believed that she was real.

In a gesture both gentle and aggressive he brushed the mother's hair, stopping intermittently to pull long gray strands out of the brush and carefully place them in his pocket.

But it was the girl who said it. And once she said it there was no taking it back.

They were in her room. They were there because it was raining. Every once in a while they would look out the window and see the honeysuckle bush, drenched and shapeless. They were playing with the dolls but really they weren't. Mostly they were sitting on the floor amidst the scattered cloth bodies wishing they were somewhere else. They hadn't been playing for a while, when the girl said it. They had been just sitting there waiting for something to happen. Then suddenly the girl said: There are ways of finding out.

She was supposed to place a piece of hot metal against the brother's skin. This was her job. If he was not her brother, then the metal would do nothing at all. It would be like maybe she was just touching him with metal that wasn't hot or maybe her hand. If he was not her brother then the not-brother would continue to sleep the whole time. It was important to do it while he was sleeping. It was necessary. Sleep was a trap. This is what the girl said. She had read all about it.

They went down the basement to look for something to use. The brother wasn't there, which seemed wrong. There was nowhere else for him to go. But if that was true and there really was nowhere else for him to go then where did he go? Outside it was still raining. Upstairs on the TV a monster movie played for no one, just the couch and the table and the dusty chairs. The basement was dark and quiet. Upstairs a beautiful woman who had been driven to kill was confronting the diabolic scientist who made her that way.

Where do you think he is? she asked.

Shh, the girl said.

The father kept his tools in a small room off of the main basement. The room seemed colder. It was definitely darker. It was lit by one light bulb hanging from the ceiling. The girls knelt in front of some boxes and rummaged around. They unpacked the boxes. The boxes were damp and unorganized. They had to pull tools out carefully, one by one. Does it have to be all metal? she whispered to the girl. The girl considered this. I think it only has to be mostly metal, she said. Eventually they settled on a screwdriver. It had a red handle and a rusty tip. Later, in her room, the girl held it against her own heart. See, the girl said.

She was ready to do it right away. But that was not how it worked. First she had to pass some tests. This was what the girl said. She had to prove that she was worthy. Plus the tests might somehow bring her brother back. Her real brother. Maybe just by enduring them something somewhere would be unlocked.

The first test was about trust. What would happen was this: the girl would do something bad. She wasn't going to say what it was, she was just going to do it. Then, when the parents found out, she would have to take the blame for whatever the girl did.

This test didn't seem like a test at all. She liked to confess. Once in school the teacher found a piece of paper with answers to an exam written all over it and asked the class to say who had done it. She stood in front of them and looked stern. For a while no one said anything. It seemed like forever. But then a little boy stood up to say that it was him, and after he did the teacher praised him. She praised him for being honest.

She looked at the boy with envy. She too wanted to confess to something. She wanted to confess and be congratulated. But there was nothing in the world she had to confess.

Now, she thought, she could confess.

So for one week she began to take the blame for everything. Any time the mother was mad about something she confessed. It wasn't easy. Sometimes she had to make up elaborate stories to connect herself to what had gone wrong. Once she and the mother came home to find the back door wide open, the kitchen chairs overturned, the trash can knocked over, and pots and pans scattered all over the floor. On the counter the blender was whirring on high. What in the hell is this! the mother exclaimed. I did it, she said. You did it, the mother said. Yes, she said, solemnly. And I'm very sorry. Would you like to explain to me how it is that you did this, the mother said. Seeing as you were with me for the past two hours. She thought for a moment. She tried to look penitent. I was keeping an animal, she said, finally. An animal, the mother said. A raccoon, she said. It was a baby, she clarified. And I was keeping her in a box in my closet and feeding it crackers. It must have escaped. The mother looked at her and sighed. Go to your room, she said.

That week she confessed to a stolen hat, a flat tire in the driveway, the neighbor's broken window, and leaving the milk out four times. Each time she hoped to be rewarded. But the mother was not the teacher. At each confession her mother got more and more upset. I don't know what you think you're doing, the mother said sternly to her one night before bed. But I can tell you with certainty that will have a lasting effect.

After a week had ended, the girls met in the lilac bush. They sat across from each other and held hands.

Which time was you? she asked the girl.

The girl's face was placid.

I never did anything, the girl said.

The second test was supposed to be a test of bravery. The girls decided she should spend the night in the woods nearby. The woods were tangled and dense. And sometimes filled with strange sounds. Rustling and buzzing and the shriek of night birds. A couple of times she had seen an older girl lead an older boy into the woods by the hand. The boy looked around like he was worried about everything. The girl, however, looked straight ahead.

It was supposed to be a test of bravery but it became something else.

All the doors in the house were locked at night, so she would have to sneak out. The best way to sneak was through the brother's room. There was a window next to the garage and from the garage she could hang down and just reach her feet to the chain-link fence below. That night, when it was time to go, she pretended to sleep. She was good at pretending. Sometimes she would lie on the couch in the living room and wait for someone to enter so she could pretend. She liked hearing them above and beyond her, completely separate from her, separate only because of her own closed eyes and her willpower. She liked knowing without being known. But it wasn't at all like being dead.

At bedtime, the mother came in to check on her. She sat next to her and absently stroked her hair. It was a rough, clawing gesture and the mother breathed loudly as she did it.

After the mother had left, she snuck out of the room. Sneaking was walking slowly and deliberately because otherwise the wood floor made creaking sounds. It was hard to determine when it would make the sounds. Sometimes even though you were sneaking the floor still made the sounds. Sometimes, she thought, it knew certain things.

At the end of the hall, the brother's door was left ajar. This was how he slept ever since he had returned. Before he had slept with it wide open. Now it couldn't be all the way open or all the way shut. She crept in on all fours. The brother was asleep in his bed. He lay inelegantly under heavy covers. In the room, it was dark. The moon wasn't up yet or there was no moon. She crept across the floor. The brother moaned a little in his sleep. He was probably sweating. She crawled to the window and opened the screen. Outside, the trees rustled. There was an electric chirring sound from some invisible insect. She turned around to look at the brother. He was sitting up in bed. He was sitting straight up and his eyes were open.

Shhh, she said to him.

He didn't say anything.

Shhh, she said again.

His eyes were wide open but they were not looking.

She got up and walked over to the bed and when she got there, he relaxed a little. He lay back down, but didn't close his eyes.

She got in bed next to him. She ran her hands through his tangled, greasy hair.

110

Shhh, she said one more time. We are sleeping, she whispered to him.

She put her arm and round him pressed herself close to his body. She could feel through his pajamas that he was cold. She could feel his breath slow down and lengthen. We are sleeping, she repeated. She said it with her eyes closed.

The next time she went again to the brother's room, it was in the daytime. The late afternoon. But still, the room was dark. The mother had pulled all the shades. Someone had. She assumed it was the mother. Who else could it be? The door to the room was half open and on the bed inside the brother lay curled into some shape. It was hard to tell if it was really him. His body was covered in blankets. But still she could make out his head, his tangle of hair.

She wasn't supposed to go to the brother's room. Now this was true. She knew she wasn't supposed to because the girl wouldn't really look at her and wouldn't come to the lilac bush, not ever, but spent her time at the kitchen table instead where she drew headless animals and talked to the mother about the color of the sky. But also there were always men in the room.

At first she didn't understand these men. One had a beard and the other didn't. They both wore sweaters and rumpled slacks. She watched them through the half-open door: there, in the brother's room, they walked around a lot and looked at things. Things in this case meant the window and the book-case and the space under the bed. When they talked to the brother, they used words like figurine and water and head. When they sat next to him on the bed, they held his hands.

She went to the room, crawling. She was an animal in the midst of some development—sniffing the air, wary. She was a night animal and she was hungry.

In the room it was only the brother. But it was dark and there were places for others to hide. At any moment the men could appear. The men in sweaters and rumpled slacks. They would appear and capture her and take her. They would take her and perform upon her rituals and tests. The rituals would be violent and possibly deadly. From them they would know the things they needed to know.

She crawled warily, creeping closer to the bed and closer, and as she crept, he disappeared from view. She got to the bed and crawled up on it. The brother's back was to her. He was lumpy, misshapen. She sat there and stared at him. Then she panted. He shifted a little but did not turn over. She panted again and nudged his head with her head. She could hear him breathing. She nudged his head again and then licked his ear. It was warm and tasted like salt.

He turned over to look at her. His eyes were filmy and distant. He smiled a little.

It's me, she said.

It's you, he said.

You don't recognize me because I'm an animal, she said.

An animal? he said.

But it's still me, she qualified.

What kind of animal? he said.

She thought for moment.

It's like a cross between a bear and an antelope, she said. It doesn't really have a name.

That's good, he said, smiling weakly at her. All the best things don't.

I'm wild, she said. But you can tame me. You can tame me by petting. What I need is to be petted.

His arms were still underneath the blankets, which were pulled up around his neck. To her he seemed restrained there, his body immobilized by the covers, weighing him down and leaving only his head free, but barely, part of some obscure punishment to redress terrible wrongs. She moved closer to him and pawed at the blanket.

Don't, he said.

She kept at her pawing.

Stop it, he said again. But his voice was not very insistent.

She stopped for a moment.

Why not? she said. This is what animals do.

I'm resting, he said. His voice sounded weird. It was soft and hoarse and a bit garbled, like something hard but also slimy was lodged in his throat.

I'm supposed to rest.

She looked at him. He was pale, anxious.

I'll help, she said. I can help.

She pulled the covers back and got in next to him.

Underneath the covers it was warm and a little damp. She lay on her back next to him, almost touching but not touching. His body was rigid. His breathing was shallow and quick.

For a while they stayed like that. But he was uncomfortable—he shifted and turned—and it made her uncomfortable.

You can't do it like that, she said, finally. You have to go limp. Otherwise it won't work. You have to close your eyes and go limp. Remember?

Here, she said.

She pulled her knees up to her chest and pulled off her baggy yellow shorts and then her underpants. She kicked them down to the bottom of the bed. Then she took off her white tank-top and threw it over the side. The bed was a raft adrift on the sea. Everything divested and thrown overboard was an offering to the tenebrous ocean and its voracious gods.

What are you doing? he said.

I'm helping, she said. See.

She unbuttoned the red flannel pajama top he was wearing.

Take it off, she said. The bottoms too.

He acted like he didn't want to. But he did it anyway.

His body was pale and skinny. Did it look like his body? She could see the outline of his ribcage pressed against his skin, like the skin had been too tightly stretched over his fragile bones. Here and there, on his arms, his chest, there were scratches and cuts.

Throw them overboard, she said.

He obeyed.

We're on a boat, she said. But it isn't just any boat. This boat is going to take you to the place you need to be. The boat is filled with flowers and stuffed animals and pictures.

Stuffed animals? he said, sitting up to look at her.

She sighed.

Because you're dead, she said. Duh. So close your eyes.

She pushed him back down into his death position.

You're dead, she said. But you're still on a journey. In books animals arrive and give you gifts. They give you gifts to help you on your way.

Gifts? he said. What gifts.

A key, a mirror, and…a cookie.

That's a gift?

It's a magical cookie, she said, matter-of-factly. Close your eyes. Be dead, she said. Now you are going to the place where the dead go. To the land beyond. It won't be easy. Once you get there, there will be tests. The important thing is to remember at all times that you are dead. They'll try to trick you into thinking you're not.

His eyes were closed and his body was relaxed. She lay back down next to him and closed her eyes too. The pyre rocked gently in the ocean. The sky was gray and the waves were gray but the horizon was a thin line of tan light. Beyond it was a king who had a deer's head for a head. He smiled and waited. He rubbed his hands.

I know you're really not my brother, she whispered to him, her eyes still shut tight. I know all about you but I won't tell.

She felt his hand touch her hand.

I won't tell, she whispered. Not for anything. And if you want to be my brother, even though I know you're not, you can.

The sky was gray and the waves were gray, but soon it would be light.

He clasped her hand in his and they lay next to each other—floating, drifting.

Across the horizon the deer-headed king smiled a cold and hungry smile.

The sky was gray, the waves were gray.

They lay there next to each other, splayed and naked.

They were just like that when they were found.

Here is what she remembers. She is sitting cross-legged underneath the kitchen table with translucent tape across her mouth. Is that right? It is night and she can see the bare white legs of her mother who is mopping the floor. It is late at night, two, maybe three. She assumes it is her mother mopping the floor. Who else could it be? On her lap she has placed a small orange pillow and on the pillow a stuffed crow. There is a sound like whispering but percussive and the mop jabs at the floor. The stuffed crow has large white glass eyes not small black ones. She calls him Henry but not to his face. Soon she will open her mouth. She will open it slowly. The tape will peel off her face, first in small bursts then all at once. It is the sensation of becoming, like pecking through a soft membrane or crawling out of a thick lake. But for a moment it will feel like she will never open her mouth again, like she has no mouth at all.

Part 3

Then she got a job taking care of women in a hospital. The hospital was an incoherent ranch-style building called the Chateau du Mons. Here the women were old but not yet dying, though they were probably closer to the great beyond than not. Sometimes they coughed and sometimes they shuddered and sometimes cried out in their sleep, but mostly they stared at the television where people talked to judges about their problems. Lucy brought them flowers, read them passages from books, and brushed with tenderness their hair. Also, she pretended to be their daughters. This didn't really entail any specific preparation or skill. Mostly, it wasn't difficult at all. Daughters, it turned out, were daughters in the end.

One day she was sitting with a woman who called her Trixie. The woman's name was Gloria Bernofsky and about Gloria one thing was true: Gloria Bernofsky did not like Trixie. When they sat together she often said things like: I always knew you would never be pretty. You weren't a pretty child. You weren't even ugly, which, at least, would have been interesting. And: Things would have been so much better if I had married that big game hunter instead of your father. Trixie, it seems, had done many things to aggrieve her mother—there were implications of harassment and petty theft; there were subtle accusations of emotional abuse—but the last straw seemed to have been leaving her in this place, where the nothing had its merry way with everyone and everything. Still though, Lucy thought, there must be some good in Trixie being here with her mother at last. But Gloria Bernofsky didn't see it this way. She didn't see it this way at all.

Today, however, was a mild day. Mrs. Bernofsky was sedate. They were playing cards and she was making certain that Mrs. Bernofsky won, even though, truthfully speaking, the woman was barely playing at all. Instead she stared at the ceiling and moved her lips like she was saying things. Lucy checked the woman's cards and then exchanged one.

Gin, she said. Again.

Stop that, Mrs. Bernofsky said. Just stop it.

Forty-five points, she said.

Oh please, Mrs. Bernofsky said and began to tear up.

Do you want to go for a swim? she asked. We could change into your bathing suit?

Mrs. Bernofsky didn't reply. Her eyes were focused on something distant. Lucy liked putting Mrs. Bernofsky in her bathing suit and had a feeling that Mrs. Bernofsky liked it too. It probably reminded her of her glamorous youth. Even though the hospital didn't have a pool, Lucy felt it was probably still a healthy activity. A kind of change of scenery. The suit was old and frilly. They would put it on and she would sit in her small bathtub. She began to unbutton Mrs. Bernofsky's blouse.

A young orderly appeared at the door.

Everything ok in here? he asked absently.

Yeah, she said. Pretty much.

Mrs. Bernofsky let out a small moan.

The orderly scanned the room and looked out the window for a moment.

Keep up the good work, he said and left.

Mrs. Bernofsky rolled over, her blouse halfway undone, and stared at the wall.

She leaned over a bit, so that she could see the side of Mrs. Bernofsky's face. For a moment though she was distracted by the woman's open shirt, the curve of her spotted breasts.

What do *you* want to do? she finally asked.

Mrs. Bernofsky closed her eyes.

Outside, later, it was overcast again. The sky portended violence. Lucy looked at it helplessly.

The young orderly was smoking near the door.

You like them, huh, he said.

What? she said.

The residents, you like them.

She looked at him for a second.

Yeah, she said. I guess.

I don't *dislike* them, he clarified. But I do think they're kind of repellent. He paused for a second and looked searchingly at the ground. They're not inviting, at least.

He took a drag off of his cigarette.

But I don't tell them that, he said. Even though sometimes I want to, I don't. You have to make them believe in themselves.

He took another long and serious drag from his cigarette.

It's the only part of the job I really like.

The sky had darkened considerably and it began to rain large cold drops. He looked at her intently, trying to make eye contact.

On her way out she had passed by a large room where a group of residents were lying face-up on the floor, their arms and legs spread out wide. They were loosely arranged in some sort of pattern. A man wearing a billowy white shirt and a manicured goatee was walking between them. You are a wonder of nature, he intoned as he went. You are part of a glorious and infinite cycle of Being, in which there is no death, only rebirth. Wheee! one tiny woman exclaimed. He walked among them and held out his hands like he was petting large animals. Breathe in, he said. And out.

When she got back to her house there was no one there. Now this was not unusual. One day she had returned home from the hospital to find the girls loading boxes into a small truck. They formed a line from the house to the street and passed their possessions one to the other.

She walked up and peered into the back of the truck. It was cavernous. The boxes filled a small dim corner. There was no furniture. No beds or appliances. She watched them silently.

What's going on, Lucy said, at last.

What does it look like? said the girl closest to her, a bit breathlessly. It's moving day.

Moving day? Lucy said.

Didn't Margo tell you, another girl said. I swore she said she told you.

We found a better house, the first girl.

I'm not sure about that, one behind her said. I mean I'm sure it's a good house, but is it necessarily better? What makes it better?

It used to be an orphanage or something, the first girl said. I mean, think of the possibilities there. Abuse, neglect, longing—it's all right there. Plus, heat's included.

I don't know. I think we could have held out. This place may have been an old Spanish consulate. Or a funeral home. Or we could have found a house that used to be a funeral home. I really don't think we were diligent enough.

She looked at the house sadly.

No one told me, Lucy said. I haven't packed. I'm not ready.

Both girls ignored her.

Your feelings on the matter are on record, the first girl said.

During the brief conversation the two had stopped putting boxes in the truck, and consequently, behind them the other girls had stopped as well. They held their boxes solemnly and waited to move again.

Where is it? she asked.

Where is what? said the girl closest to her.

Our new place, she said.

Seriously? the girl said. She didn't seem annoyed, just honestly incredulous.

She didn't know how to answer this question, what it was supposed to mean.

I just, she said after a moment, I have to get boxes and borrow a car and...

The girls looked at each other.

Lucy, Lucy, the girl said and for a few seconds it seemed like she didn't know what else to say, that this was all there was to say.

You're not moving, she said. *We're* moving. You're not... part of it. I mean, I'm sure you'll agree that while there is something endearing about you, there is also something deeply unsettling. You're uneasy. It's not pleasant. It suited us here. Here it was great. In this house, the girl looked back at it with some emotion, you were perfect. But we don't think it's going to help us elsewhere. I mean, this house, she continued, with its strangely articulated rooms and damp basement, well, I can tell you, we knew right away that you were the one. You completed the whole experience. It was like finding the perfect couch to match the curtains. Or a table, she said excitedly. Like finding an end table that you've always dreamed about and one day on the street, there it is, just sitting there, as if it had been waiting just for you, all its life, as if some benevolent god had been guiding you the whole time.

Like Jason, said the second girl. Over the ocean.

The first girl ignored her.

Only to discover, she said, that, in the end, it's just not what you wanted. Maybe one leg is shorter than the other. Maybe the top is nicked. It's not that we didn't have hopes. We all had hopes. I don't think our hopes themselves could have been higher. But in any case, she said, brightly, when beginning a new adventure, it's best to start fresh. I'm quite positive we'll find what we need for our new home.

Lucy looked around at the girls. They all stood still. Some looked at the ground; others at the trees, the houses, the occasional animal. Some looked directly her, but kind of blankly. They held their boxes tightly.

Which one is Margo? she asked.

You know, you were always funny, the girl said. At least there's that.

For a while after the girls left, the house was either a tomb or tableau. Lucy walked from room to room trying to come to some sort of understanding of her new situation. Now it is just me and the house, she thought. She didn't know if this was a comforting thought.

Where there were still beds, she tried out the beds, and where there weren't any beds, she laid on the floor. Mostly the house was empty. The girls had left some things behind, but not much. A dresser, a chair, a few lumpy mattresses. Sometimes there were sounds, the wind, maybe, or maybe something else. A scratching-like, a restlessness. She thought: The rooms don't look like rooms. The house doesn't seem like a house. It was more like a puzzle without instructions, an unmarked package left on your doorstep.

But then again maybe, she thought, that *was* a house. Maybe a house wasn't things. Maybe it was sounds, sounds always there, but unnoticed because of other sounds. Like walking and breathing. But now there were no other sounds to hear. There was only the house in all it's empty purity.

This thought unnerved her.

She decided to make a plan. She would remake the whole thing. She drew the rooms and what should go in them: the dressers, the tables, the beds, the carpets; the shoes, the jackets, the dresses and hats. Each object was a simple shape that corresponded to another shape on another piece of paper, which she kept but didn't look at. She did this alone, in her own room, in the darkness of her own room. She sat on the floor and imagined the rest of the house, room by room.

When the plan was complete, she began to move the things into their rooms. First she used anything the girls left behind, then she went out looking. This was mostly at night. During the day, when she wasn't working, she slept in long almost feverish bouts, in which she dreamt that she wasn't sleeping at all but waking periodically to the sounds of dogs and lawnmowers. At night she went through people's things without them knowing. Everywhere now people were leaving their things in front of their houses. Furniture, clothing, dishware. She combed through them meticulously to find the best approximation of a yellow dress or the perfect number of scratches on a table. The houses and apartments were dark or mostly dark. Sometimes there was a light in a window.

When the house was done, she could go into any room she wanted. She could breathe. But even still she heard the sounds. When she closed her eyes she could hear them and when she opened her eyes she could hear them and now it was mostly a clicking sound—click, click, click, like an long-clawed animal scuttling across the floor.

The next day was her day to take the women for a walk. "Touring" is what this was called. The idea, the head nurse explained to her, was to activate latent mental and physical attributes without over stimulating them. Patients, the head nurse said, needed the illusion of control. For this reason there was a dog involved. The patient at the head of the line was given the responsibility of walking the hospital dog and everyone else had to fall in line behind the walker. It was not a responsibility idly assigned. Every day patients won the honor. They won it through compliance. They took their pills; they ate all their applesauce; they used the toilet convincingly—in short, they demonstrated they were very good patients indeed. The winner would concentrate on walking the dog while the other patients would concentrate on the dog they wished they were walking. In this way, they could avoid any unpleasant interactions with the world they were supposed to be enjoying.

Today's winner was Mrs. Upton. Unfortunately for her, Mrs. Upton was allergic to dogs. She stood at the head of the line holding the leash gingerly and eyeing the animal with fear. Every so often the poor women would sneeze violently. Walking a dog was the last thing Mrs. Upton wanted to do.

I'll bet we can get someone else to do it, Lucy told Mrs. Upton reassuringly and went to talk to the head nurse about it.

The head nurse, however, was adamant.

My dear, the head nurse said. We can do nothing of the sort.

She was a broad, imposing woman with severely cropped sandy hair and a tight, expressionless face.

The rules are the rules, she continued. They are not recommendations. They are not suggestions. You must learn to think of them as closer to immutable natural laws. And rule number one, the primary rule from which all others spring, is walking the hospital dog.

She stared incomprehensibly at the head nurse.

But then it's not much of a prize, she said.

Oh sweetheart! the nurse said consolingly. Winning doesn't always equal pleasure. My goodness, it's like you've never encountered logic a day in your life! If the day's winner doesn't walk the dog, well, I don't even want to think about what could happen. Anyone can walk the dog at any time! Or not walk the dog! Or decide to go naked! Or play in their own filth! My dear, the very foundation of the hospital rests on the winner doing her job. The head nurse leaned in close. Her perfume was unctuous and overpowering. Whether she wants to, the nurse said firmly, or not.

The tour was, generally speaking, a solemn affair. Lucy led the dog and the dog led the walker and the walker led the group. For a block or two they would exercise their capacities and then return to the safety of the hospital. No one really spoke to each other. No one really looked around. At first, today was no different. Mrs. Upton led the way, coughing, sneezing, and making occasional gagging sounds. Mrs. Lunt wore a towel draped over her head. To protect herself, she said. Mrs. Tsai shook her head slightly from side to side and occasionally muttered something about a red pencil. The rest of the women walked with desultory focus. They made their allotted turn. But when they arrived at the corner where it was usual for them to turn around and go back, Lucy kept them walking. She walked right across the street and onto the next block. She didn't say anything. She just did it. Behind her she could hear them women begin to talk excitedly in voluble bursts. After a few minutes she stopped and relieved a grateful Mrs. Upton of her duties and handed them over to Mrs. Buttersby, who at first seemed hesitant to take the lead but warmed considerably as they went, straightening her back and yanking on the leash with confidence. They continued on in this way, walking and stopping occasionally to switch the lead, the women now talking with each other, laughing, as they went. Ella, the hospital dog, was stoic about her new situation. She was used to being handled by different people. Back at the hospital she had free reign to do as she pleased. She ghosted the halls, poking her head into patients' rooms, doctors' offices, and lounges. Every room treated her with the solemn joy accorded to an arriving dignitary.

Eventually they came to a large empty field that seemed to mark the end of the neighborhood. The field was about maybe a hundred yards or so. It was filled with high grasses and tiny flowers. At the other end was a brand new development. In the middle was a big sign that read Future Home of Lost Woods Estates.

Lucy looked the field over dispassionately. Well, I suppose it's time to turn around, she said.

The women appeared upset.

Do we have to? Mrs. Tsai said quietly.

Maybe, Mrs. Upton, said. We could have a picnic?

How are we going to have a picnic without food? Mrs. Lunt grumbled.

I have some crackers I took from the cart at lunch, Mrs. Buttersby offered.

That's hardly what I'd call a picnic, Mrs. Lunt said.

Let's pretend we just finished eating and now it's time to rest and play games, Mrs. Atterak said.

They all looked at Lucy, except for Mrs. Lunt who looked at Mrs. Buttersby. Are you going to eat those crackers? she asked.

They all waded out into the field together. They moved in a snaking line, each woman holding on to another's hand for balance and guidance, holding gently but firmly as they moved through the high grass, through the small flowers, giggling and pulling at each other, until they came to the very center of the field. There they tamped down the grass and flowers into a clearing. Lucy helped each woman sit down. And they stared up at the sky out of the circle they had made.

The sky was blue and the sun was hot. The women were happy in their little circle. Each seemed to remove herself a little bit from the company to consider her own abilities and fortunes. Mrs. Galk muttered something about cheese and Mrs. Atterak counted on her fingers; Mrs. Tsai said

"Bunting!" and then laughed and then was silent; Mrs. Lunt had her head on Mrs. Buttersby's lap and was sleeping quietly while Mrs. Buttersby stroked Mrs. Lunt's hair and hummed a meandering tune; Mrs. Upton stared up at the sky and its implications.

Then suddenly the afternoon storms swept in. Gigantic dark and whirling clouds filled the sky. There was a huge cracking noise. Ella whined and began to pull at the leash. She pulled left, then right, left, then right. Mrs. Galk, who had gathered Ella up for the return trip, was having a hard time holding on. The sky cracked again and Ella bolted, yanking the surprised Mrs. Galk to the ground.

Shit, said. Lucy.

The dog! said Mrs. Upton.

My ankle! Mrs. Galk whimpered. My ankle!

Lucy got up and ran after Ella for a few seconds, but the dog had sprinted into the development. It hopped right over the fence. The other women were helping Mrs. Galk off the ground.

I think it's broken, said Mrs. Buttersby.

Mrs. Galk was crying loudly.

Jesus, she sobbed. Jesus Christ.

It's going to be ok, said Lucy.

My goodness, Darling, Mrs. Atterak said, patting Mrs. Galk on the arm, it's not as bad as all that.

I'll go get Ella and then I'll call for the van.

You'll dance again, my dear, Mrs. Atterak told her. You'll be up in no time and doing the Watusi.

Mrs. Galk's sobs turned into gulps and sniffles and they all looked at her with tenderness.

Just wait here, Lucy told them. I'll be right back.

She ran toward the development.

Following the fence Lucy called after the dog until she came to the development's entrance. An older man was sitting outside a booth reading a book.

She stood there in front of the gate for a moment, shuffling her feet, and waiting to be recognized. The guard, however, was enthralled with his book.

Excuse me, she said at last.

Oh, he said, looking at her over, appraisingly. We don't want any.

What? she said.

We're not interested, he said.

No, she said. I mean…I'm not selling anything.

Are you sure? he asked.

Of course, she said.

Because it would be terrible to find out that you were selling something you didn't even know you were selling.

What? she said.

Insurance? he asked.

No.

Well-being?

I'm looking, she said.

A fine collection of kitchen knives?

For a dog, she finished.

A dog! he exclaimed. He looked mildly alarmed. That's not possible, he said, firmly. Dogs are not allowed.

It jumped the fence, she said.

I hardly think that's feasible, the guard said.

It was over on the side by the field, she said.

That *is* perplexing, he said. He knitted his already wrinkled brow together. Are you sure about the knives? he asked.

Please, she said. It's not my dog. I just take care of it and if I don't get it back. Lucy paused. She didn't even know what would happen if she couldn't find the dog.

The guard sighed. He got up and walked into the booth. He pressed a button and then came out and manually opened the gate.

Come on, he said.

Together they walked into the development. The development wasn't distinctive in any way. Each house looked like another house. The streets curled back on each other and bifurcated into radials. Lucy kept thinking she caught Ella out of the corner of her eye but when she turned to really see her, the dog wasn't there. Ella, she called out plaintively. Ella.

The guard walked unsteadily beside her.

Looking can be a difficult business, he said. Yep. Sometimes I say to myself, Belvedere—that's me—Belvedere, I say, the world only has one face. But it's the kind of face that looks like other faces.

He looked at her with expectation.

Depending on the angle, he clarified.

Ella, she called out again. Ella

Course that's just one way to look at it, he went on. My wife Rosy would say, "Why try to make jelly out of jam?" She's for a certain amount of ignorance. "The unlidded eye is both uncharacteristic and vulnerable." That's another of hers. But I'm in security, I tell her. It's my job to regard minutiae with tenderness.

Here, Ella, she said.

I'll tell you something else. Places like this, boy, they make it hard. There's something sinister about these what-do you-call-them...developments. They resist speculation. Personally I think they're designed to encourage oblivion. But that's just a theory. Any luck with your doggy?

She sighed.

Dogs, he said, shaking his head. Who can know their feral minds?

Maybe we could get some help, she said.

Help is always a fine thing, Belvedere mused.

Maybe we should ask someone, she volunteered.

Ask someone? Belvedere chuckled. Sure. Why not. Go ahead.

She looked around. All the houses seemed empty. There were no cars in any driveways and no children's toys left out on the lawns

Is everyone at work? she asked.

Work! Belvedere exclaimed. Work! He laughed and laughed until the laughs became cough. The coughs were phlegmy, rattling coughs that racked him until he leaned over and spit.

I don't understand, she said.

You sure don't, Belvedere said, cheerfully, still leaning over. He spit again. But that's nothing to be ashamed about. Here, there's nothing, nothing but nothing, he said. Every single house empty. Look around. Every place just a desolate temple, waiting for its own personal family to love it up.

Lucy walked over to one of the houses and peered into the big bay window. Inside, the room was a tastefully decorated living room and dining room. She could make out a long wooden table and attendant chairs, a low white sofa that looked uncomfortable, a coffee table that resembled some sort of antique chest. There was even artwork on the walls— large soft-focus photographs of natural wonders designed to encourage easy relaxation and self-satisfaction. Belvedere sidled up next to her and shared the view.

You know, he said, softly. Sometimes I look at these houses and think to myself—Belvedere, there's a whole world right here. A whole invisible world.

His breathing was shallow and rapt.

I heard this story once, he said. It was about this town that got swallowed up by a lake. Swallowed whole. What do you make of that?

He paused for a moment to cough again and clear his throat.

I'll tell you what, he continued. I thought it was about the craziest thing I ever heard. Well this town, such as it was, was situated on an island in the middle of the lake I'm talking about. Lake Oswego? Lake Takawami? Some Indian name or other. I'm terrible about names. Just terrible. But anyway, this town had been there for years. *Hundreds* of years. It was a real piece of the American puzzle, this place, a bona fide nail in the original scaffolding. The people that grew up there, they could trace their families back to, well, who even knows. Trappers and blacksmiths and farmers of sheep. The older professions, the work of dignity. Anyway, one winter it rained. It rained and rained. Instead of snowing, that's all it did. Right through the winter and into the spring. And then it kept on going. A mild winter, it's something to fear. That's one of my momma's. Anyway, so, because of all the rain, the water on the lake rose and kept rising. It rose and rose until one thing became clear: the people would have to leave. This wasn't a realization that came easily. Generally speaking realizations come about as easy as a rusty nail out of a car fender. But where homes are concerned? Holy moly! Let me tell you. I guard these things every day. You can bet it took a while for people pry their poor hands loose. But in the end, everybody did it. They all left. The gathered their belongings and floated away. A few—I'm sure—had to be knocked over the head and just dragged onto those boats. Figuratively speaking, of course. You know how it is with leaving. But in the end everyone got out and just barely. Not even a year and the whole island disappeared. And it remained like that. A perfect lake. A mirror. Years on and people just forgot about it entirely, the island, the town, like they do. It became a place of entertainment, this lake. Folks went swimming; they went boating. They *capered* there. And all the time unaware that underneath them a whole town was still there, waiting. You'd think, Belvedere said, that a lake like that would be the focus of a lot of, let's just say, less than ruly energy. Something untoward and sinister. I don't know what you believe but to me that seems sensible. But if you thought that, you, like me, would be wrong. Nothing ever happened. No mysterious accidents. No strange weather. It was just another lake. Just one more watery vacation spot to fill out the allotted time. But then many years later—what? eighty? ninety?—there was a drought, a drought as dry as the flood had been wet, and slowly the water level dropped, revealing for the first time the town that had once been the lake's very heart. People came from miles around. They waded across the shallows to see this snapshot of a town. Their own personal Pompeii. I'm sure it was marvelous to behold. And solemn. Anyway, sometimes that's how I imagine these houses. Like something frozen in time. Except these are the future. Can you get your head around that?

Belvedere absently scratched his temple. It's a sad story all right, he said. A real tear-jerker. But that's the way of all things.

Although I may have read about it in a book.

Can we go in and look around? Lucy asked.

Honey, there's only so much I can do for you, Belvedere said, a bit coolly.

Just then it finally began to rain. For a moment she had forgotten about the sky and its clouds. She had forgotten about Ella and the women and the whole illicit outing. It was the houses and the streets, curving, anodyne, repetitive, plus maybe Belvedere himself that had conspired to distract her, dissolve her, pull her through the skin of one life into another.

Oh shit, she said.

What? Belvedere said, looking around him with care.

The women, she said.

What women? Belvedere said.

I'm responsible for a bunch of sick women, she hastily explained

I thought it was a dog, said Belvedere.

It is a dog, she said.

Well hell, Belvedere said. Make up your mind.

She didn't say anything but turned around and ran.

Be right back, she yelled over her shoulder.

Behind her Belvedere stood in the pouring rain. He stared blankly, surrounded by his ghostly charges.

When she got back to the field, all the women were gone. She looked wildly around her. Where had they gone? How? Lucy started running back to the hospital, back the way they had come. Mrs. Upton? she yelled. Mrs. Billingsly? The rain came steadily down, blurring everything. She knocked on the door of first house but no one answered. She crossed the street and knocked on another. No answer. She looked around helplessly. They must have found somewhere to go, somewhere warm and dry. The best thing to do was wait it out herself and then come back to the field and hope they came back too. When she was little her mother always said, When you're lost just stay where you are and eventually we'll find you, though often it never happened that way and a security had to call her mother's name over the intercom over and over until she, mortified, arrived to claim her. Lucy walked back through the rain the way they had all come. She was soaked. Freezing. She stopped at a convenience store a block away. The store was bright and ice cold. The air was running high. The only person in the store was the clerk, a middle-aged bald man with a beard, who grimaced at her as she entered and then returned to watching a small TV behind the counter.

She looked at the magazines for a few minutes, pretending to be a customer. Car magazines, rock magazines, magazines about near naked men that fought other men. She flipped through them idly. On the top rack the coifed heads of blandly seductive women grew like flowers from the black plastic shields obscuring their bodies. They stared at her, past her, waiting. She returned to the window and the storm, its preternatural darkness. Rain thudded against the shop windows.

Hey you, the clerk called from behind her. Little miss browser. Little miss not-gonna-buy. You want a hot chocolate?

She turned to look at him. Now he was standing up, behind the counter, at attention, a cup in his hand.

Have a hot chocolate, he said, putting the cup down the counter. It's a mess out there and you sure look like you could use it.

He smiled.

She walked over to the register, took the cup and looked into it. The liquid was dark and purplish-tan. The aroma thin and cloying. It certainly seemed like hot chocolate. She took a sip. The liquid slid over her tongue and into her throat. It's heat spread. She shivered

Thanks, she said and took another sip.

Buck fifty, he said.

She looked at him. The look said: really?

Everything in its rightful place, the clerk said. He had reassumed the placid, disinterested face of his profession.

She sighed, put the cup on the counter, stepped back from it.

I don't have my wallet on me, she said. But I work at the Chateau down the street. I can get it when the storm ends.

I'm just kidding, he said. He opened up his mouth into a smile again. He pushed the cup back to her. This poor, wet, bedraggled thing.

But I'll tell you what, he said. You could do something for me anyway. Let's call it a payment. Kindness for kindness.

Why don't you let me take your picture? Let me take your picture and we'll call it even.

My picture? she said.

It's nothing weird, he said. I'm not a weirdo. I'm just a collector is all. I collect faces. Nothing like a good face. It's rejuvenating. A good face. A face that tells a story. It makes the whole day worthwhile. And let me tell you something: I've seen a lot of faces—in this job it's nothing but—and you have one—I wish you could see yourself—spectacular countenance.

She felt the heat of his attention rise in her armpits, her neck and cheeks. She looked down at the counter, the floor.

I gotta say, it's one of the most exquisitely sad faces I've ever seen. I mean, you're the goddamned Mona Lisa of melancholy.

She looked at him again. He seemed excited, earnest, almost pleading.

C'mon, he said. The hot chocolate, plus refills, plus a towel to dry yourself off, he said.

Ok, she said. Fine

The clerk directed Lucy over to the brick wall next to the office door. He kept a respectful distance the whole time, a good five feet. She leaned against the wall and he lifted the camera to his face.

Ok, he said. Just think about nothing.

Think about nothing.

Yeah, nothing. Something without any kind of emotion attached to it. Like eating a sandwich.

Ok, she said.

But not one you really like. Maybe just a cheese sandwich.

I get it, she said.

One without mustard, he added.

Lucy stood against the wall and stared straight ahead.

That's great, he said. The camera clicked a bunch of times.

See, he told her. No big deal.

Wanna take a look?

Lucy shrugged.

He turned the camera around and pulled up a photo of her. Against the brick wall a young woman stood and stared. Her face was pale. Her eyes were small and narrow. That was her? That was her face? The strange face stared implacably back.

Hey, he said, leaning in close. Hey, he whispered. I got a better deal for you. If you take off your top and pretend to cry, you can have anything you want in the store.

When she got back to the Chateau, she went first to the locker room to change. She would get out of her wet clothes and then get the hospital van. She would drive around until she found them.

She had taken off her cold wet hospital scrubs and was standing in her underwear, rubbing her arms, when the head nurse walked in. Deftly, without turning around, she locked the door behind her.

Here you are, the nurse said. I've been looking everywhere.

I'm so sorry, Lucy began.

Of course you are, my dear, the head nurse cut her off. Of course you are. But you'll be happy to know that everyone is fine. A little bit wet and a little bit shaken. But, for the most part, fine. We had the doctors looking them over as soon as they came in and we've been assured that there is no real damage to speak of. But in general: Catastrophe averted.

That's good, she said softly.

It's fantastic! said the head nurse, gaily. The ever-enterprising Mrs. Buttersby was in secret possession of a cell phone, if you can believe that, which she used to call for rescue. Of course we've confiscated the nasty device and docked her dessert for a month. But without it, who knows where we'd be! A little lesson in consequences for you.

The nurse sat down on the bench in front of the lockers and vigorously patted the space next to her. Lucy sat down and the nurse immediately put her hand on Lucy's naked leg. The hand, hot and rough, tightened around her thigh.

Although, the head nurse said a bit more gravely, it's not all good news. We are, you are aware, missing one hospital dog. I'm sure I don't have to tell you the importance of that dog. What it means to both patients and staff. Did you know that Dr. Hagens picked that dog out himself for the very purpose it now serves? He's written papers on that thing. He carries her picture in his wallet. A proud papa. Thank goodness he's on vacation. Who's to say what would happen? The kinds of things he would do? But I'm sure it will all work out in the end.

I'll find her, Lucy said, miserably. I'll be better. I'll do my best.

Oh no, the head nurse said. No you won't. I've seen your best. I've watched it unfold, tethered, as it is, to delusions of insight and propriety. My word! You're like an unattended garden hose, spraying everything but the vegetables! No, no, my dear. What you'll do now is *my* best. What you'll do now is exactly what you are told. You've had your chance and it turned out terribly. Now, the nurse said cheerfully, it's time to grow up.

For the next few weeks Lucy stayed away from the hospital. She couldn't face the head nurse and she couldn't face the women. She had gone back to the development and looked for Ella the dog. She had walked carefully around the whole community and looked in every yard and under every bush and still found nothing. You know, Belvedere had said. I think what it is, is that sometimes dogs just turn right into dreams. For no dang reason.

One day the young orderly appeared at the house. It took her a while to recognize him. He stood at the threshold of her room and didn't say anything and didn't come in.

Lucy looked at him.

The door was open, he said. Downstairs it was open.

She continued to look. Who knows how long he may have been standing there looking at her? She couldn't tell if this was a reassuring thought.

I knocked several times, he said. But no one answered. He stepped tentatively into the room. I brought you some orange juice, he said and held out the small carton of orange juice like he was coaxing a stray.

Thanks, she said, but didn't move.

They said you were sick, he said, looking around. But you don't look sick. Which is good, he added. I guess.

I'm dealing with some things, she said.

Oh, he said. Well, that's good. Better to deal than let them build up and fester.

Just then a woman began wailing dramatically. It was a record. She had been listening to records she had bought because she liked the covers, and on this one a woman was wailing dramatically and incoherently. She was accompanied by someone playing one piano key over and over and over.

The orderly looked alarmed.

What the hell is that?

Lucy nodded towards the record player.

It's the music, she said.

The music, he said.

It's this, she said and handed him the sleeve, though she didn't really want to. Somehow she felt protective of the sleeve. On it a woman with wild dark hair and garish makeup, clearly in the throes of passion, but somehow also contemplative and sad, was being held by unseen hands.

The orderly fingered it carelessly.

You like this? he said.

She considered the question, which wasn't in fact a question at all. The things that are not what they appear to be.

I guess I don't, he said after a while. Not really. I wanted to say that I did. It was the first thing that occurred to me to say. That way we could share something immediately. But I decided against it, which I think was the right course. I decided to be honest.

He smiled.

You like it though, he said a bit sadly.

Now just the one piano key, poorly tuned, in between oceans of hissing silence.

It reminds me of something, Lucy said, quietly. Something I can't place.

That's the problem with this kind of stuff, he said, suddenly and with urgency. It's all random associations and incoherent feelings. Some of them may not even be real.

He stared at the sleeve again with distaste, rubbing his free hand against his jeans.

Personally I don't care for it, he said.

You don't "care for it"? she said, incredulous.

I don't mind it, the orderly said. But I don't consider myself an aficionado. I prefer messages, he said. Thoughts and opinions. I like books on tape. Two, three at a time. I'm reading one right now about activating your inner Spartan and another one about getting the prosperity you deserve. I think you'd like them.

Now on the record the woman was softly chanting something about rats. Rats in the streets, she chanted. Wearing human feet.

For a while they just looked at each other and at the room and at each other. There was something else here with them. Lucy could feel it. She could feel it the minute the orderly had stepped across the threshold. Suddenly, the room, this room, her room, had become another room, rearranged quite subtly around the orderly's presence. In the corner by the book shelf there was a big dust bunny. The paint on the windowsill was flaking and chipping. It hadn't looked like this yesterday. Or even this morning. All that dark matter no one knows what to do with, Lucy thought but couldn't make the thought connect. She pulled her shorts towards her knees in quick tugs.

They found it, he said after a while.

The dog, he clarified.

Oh, she said. That's good.

It was living for a while in a bar with this guy Duke, he told her. Duke was feeding her cheeseburgers and mayonnaise. She was a real horror show when she came back. But she's been on an exercise regime. Two walks a day. She's getting back to fighting shape.

Fighting, she said.

He looked at Lucy with tenderness and also something else.

It's an expression, he said.

I know, she said and then quickly felt uncomfortable for saying it.

The woman on the record was no longer singing about rats. In fact she wasn't singing at all. The needle of the record player bumped with desultory insistence against the record's end.

I followed you home, the orderly said, softening his voice. One day. I followed you home. You intrigue me. You're...uneasy. So I followed you home. It's not a creepy thing. It's not meant to be. I didn't think you'd mind. You don't seem like the kind of person who would mind. Like maybe you'd even find it charming.

He paused for a moment.

And it was only to the end of the block, anyway. So I could see where you lived. Not how you lived. I'm not a weirdo. I was just…interested. Anyway, that's how I knew where to find you.

I was assaulted that day, he said. I was standing there at the end of the block and this guy comes up to me right next to me, looking where I'm looking. Nice evening, he says. Sure is, I say. Got a cigarette, he says. Nope, I say. Good for you, he says. And then hits me, full in the face. He may have had brass knuckles because my lip split right open. When I came to, he was just standing over me. He didn't take anything or try something. He was just standing there, staring at me. And then walks away. He could've killed me. I could be dead. Who knows how long I was out? But he just stood there and then walked away.

So I go to the hospital. I got forty stitches. Here and here, he said pointing to parts of his lip and cheek. It hurt for days.

That's, she said, pausing for a moment. Terrible, she concluded.

That's not the real terrible thing. I mean shit happens. Right? The real terrible thing was this: a week or so ago I finally got around to washing the clothes I was wearing. For a while I didn't want anything to do with them. *They scared me*, those clothes. I didn't even hide them. They were balled up in a corner of the room. Sometimes I didn't sleep in the room. Because of those clothes. I avoided my own room because of the clothes. But at some point I thought: I'm not going to be a victim anymore. These clothes have no power over me. So I decided to wash them. When I was emptying out the pockets I found a note. A handwritten note. It said: You are loved. It was from the guy. The guy put in my pocket while I was unconscious, he said. And he signed it. From Big George, the note said.

Jesus, she said, because she didn't know what else to say.

He looked at her thoughtfully and intently. You know, it took a lot of courage to come back here, I think. To face those fears. I'm even wearing the clothes I wore that day.

Lucy looked him over. He was wearing stiff blue jeans and a red T-shirt. They didn't seem to have ever been worn, let alone party to psychological terror.

Do you mind if I sit next to you? he said, and then abruptly sat next to her. She could feel his arm slightly graze her arm. He looked at her. She looked at the floor. He looked around the room.

I like you, he said. I think we're going to be friends.

The orderly stayed up late and soon so did she. They listened to the radio and he read her passages from his books. The books were about as interesting as she expected. But he was clearly nuts for them. He approached them like sacrament. "The true warrior finds little use in cultivated mystery," the orderly read to her solemnly. "He is alert to the clarity of the manifold world." She tried to listen to these words but they were difficult to get a hold of. They squirmed away from her as if repelled. Was this what it meant to be in love?

One night he told her about his mother. His mother, he said, was not well. She had always been unwell, at least as long as he could remember. She lay in bed a lot. She didn't sleep. She just lay there and stared at the ceiling. Sometimes he crawled in next to her. Under the covers he wrapped his arm and legs around her body, which was hot and kind of moist and unresponsive. But this wasn't to say that she was not also sometimes well. Once she took him out of school to go to the movies. She arrived and told the principal that there had been a death in the family. In the darkness of the theater they sat side by side and watched a shirtless, muscled man defend a broken kingdom with a magic sword and some animal friends. She put her hand on his and interlaced their fingers. On the screen a tiger licked the man's sweaty, wounded chest.

But at a certain point, he said, she became more unwell than well. When he was seventeen they had to put her in a hospital. Five days later she called from a pay phone. She had escaped from the hospital, she said, because it was a terrible place. There were patients everywhere! But mom, he said into the phone, it's a hospital. You don't understand, his mother said. The patients just walked around doing whatever they wanted. This is what she meant by everywhere. One had opened up the door to her room, her own private room. He opened the door and after doing so he stood there looking at her and masturbating. It might have been a doctor, she said. You can't really tell in that place. In any case, she said. He reminded me of you.

Now she appeared and disappeared. He was unsure where she went when she went and equally unsure why she came back. Sometimes, I wish she wouldn't, he said. But I know that she always will.

As he spoke Lucy looked at him and she didn't. She let her eyes move to his arms and his Adam's apple and lose focus. She imagined gently grabbing his head and placing it between her legs. There she could pet it like something small and orphaned.

Some time later the mother was there in the house. She was asleep on the couch, her back to the room. She was a bony woman wearing baggy clothes. She had long stringy hair the color of standing water. Her breathing was fitful and deep. Just like the orderly's breathing. This was how Lucy knew it was the mother and how she knew the mother was there to stay.

The mother didn't do much. Mostly she slept and watched TV. Although she didn't really watch TV as much as just stare at it. She smoked cigarettes and sat on the couch while judges talked to people about their problems. She also cooked. Sometimes the whole house would begin to smell of something mildewed and old. This is how she knew the mother was cooking. The mother only made food in a large pot that she brought with her. It was gray and battered and had strange dark spots all over it. The food was also gray, a watery brown-gray stew of some kind with chunks of tough vegetables and stringy meat. Eat, the mother would say, staring at Lucy until she did.

But then, one day, the mother spoke to her, really spoke.

I bet you think it's always like this, the mother said. This was in the front room. The room with the TV.

Lucy was just leaving, walking out the door, when the mother called out to her and she turned around.

The mother was nursing a cup of murky tea.

I bet you think, the mother continued, that it is forever the mother on the couch. Sleeping, not sleeping, it is all the same.

No, she said. It's not like that.

What is it like? the mother said.

I don't know, she said.

What *do* you know? the mother said.

I, she said, helplessly.

Exactly, the mother said.

The room was dark. It was always dark. Her eyes, the mother said, they were sensitive. She said this and stared. For too long she stared, her eyes deep set and watery, her face yellow, thin, and loose. On the TV several people sat in a dingy white room and admitted to each other they were powerless over their behaviors. This was where the puppet shows had been. But now there was only this: the mother, the TV, the people, the darkness. There was also the smell. There was that too.

I will tell you what you know, the mother said after a while. She spoke quietly and forcefully. You know that here is a man. He is not sometimes, what is the word, steady. He goes here, he goes there. He has ideas. Who has ideas? These days who can afford them? But still he is this: a man. He has warm hands and he cares for you. This is enough. But let me tell you something. Hands don't hold one thing for all eternity. They are busy. Busy hands, always grasping, always looking for the perfect grip. This is not you. I know these things. I am the mother. This is not you.

This was in the room where the puppet shows had been. Sometimes Lucy sat in the room alone, though not often. If the mother wasn't there, she soon would be. But this is the way it was in the house. Each room was now, in some way, the mother's. Each room was hard to keep clean.

Later, she told the orderly about this and he told her the following story.

You'll notice, he said, that mother is missing two fingers on her left hand. This, he told her, was from when she was a girl. She had been raised, it turned out, in the middle of some terrible conflict in another country. In this country there were two groups, who were basically indistinguishable and had for years lived next to each other. They had eaten with each other and intermarried and borrowed from each other. But suddenly, after a change in political regime, they decided that they hated each other and claimed that they had always hated each other and that the whole previous history had been an enforced charade. Then they began to try to kill as many of each other as possible. This happened all over the country. Even in the smallest villages, of which the mother's was one. The mother's brother was particularly convinced of the new reality and keen to participate. But their father wouldn't let him. The father said: This afternoon we were brothers and it will be so again tomorrow. Today is the merely a night of bad dreams. The brother didn't listen. One day the father found him with a bunch of boys throwing rocks at a small girl who was part of the other group. He carried him home and scolded him severely. Still the brother didn't listen. They are not like us, the brother said, defiantly. They are barely human. The father looked at him with sadness and disappointment. Finally he said, Take a look at your mother. Is she not human? The brother was horrified. He locked himself in the bathroom with the water running for a day and a half. When he finally emerged he was taciturn but repentant. He apologized to their father. He hugged their mother. He ate dinner with the family. Everything was right again. But that night he woke his sister, the orderly's mother, in the middle of the night. He slipped into her bed and stared at her until she woke. Then he took her to the barn. He put her hand flat against the of an old tree stump. He took out a large knife and said: We will remove the parts of ourselves that are impure. He gripped her wrist tightly and cut down first on her pinky and then her ring finger. He did not need to silence her. She swallowed her cries because she loved her brother. After he had finished, the brother tenderly wrapped the fingers in white swaddling and asked for her other hand. She just had placed it upon the stump, when suddenly the father appeared in a rage. He grabbed the brother by the arm and yanked him away from the stump. With his free hand, the brother tried to stab the father, but the father easily batted away the knife. He held the brother there, wriggling in impotent rage. You are not a man, the father said. What kind of man does this to a little girl? You are not even a bad man. A bad man, at least, would have succeeded. You are nothing, the father spat. He threw the brother out of the barn and the brother ran sobbing and crying, screaming hateful things into the woods. She never saw him again, her brother. For a long time his mother hated her father for this, the orderly said. And said she would never ever forgive him.

So you see, the orderly said. You can't really blame her.

They were in bed. The mother was in the circular room with the curtains pulled. The orderly pressed himself against her, his leg over her leg, and held her own fingers loosely in his hand. He rubbed them absently and kissed her hair.

Of course, she said, of course.

But she couldn't see why not.

And then for a week afterwards she had this dream. It wasn't a recurring dream. It was one dream that unfolded over the course of many nights. In the dream she was a child and she was playing alone in her room in the house by the sea. She played with her porcelain-faced dolls, dressing them and undressing them. After she was done she went to put the dolls where she put all her toys: into the head of this giant green plastic frog. The whole thing was just head. A head with feet. It had hinges on the back that made it crack wide open. She liked to crack open the head and rummage around inside it, arranging and rearranging her dolls and other toys. She didn't do this in the dream, but she knew about it and that she must do it, that it was important. However, when she got to the frog's head she found there was no way to open it. What had previously very clearly been two pieces of green plastic attached by the hinge was now uninterrupted and smooth. She walked back and forth it running her fingers over the smooth plastic where the mouth had been. It was horrible and wrong! She looked at the dolls strewn all over the floor and became agitated. The dolls had to be put away. They couldn't be left out. What would happen to them if they weren't put in their place? They were her responsibility! What would happen to her? The frog's face suddenly seemed sinister. It was grinning like it knew what it was doing. It was mocking her. She looked at her dolls. They were grinning too. She took one in her hand. She didn't know what else to do. She began to beat on the top of the frog's head with the porcelain-faced doll. She beat and beat until the head broke wide open. It shattered like it was glass, not plastic. Little green shards. On the top of the head there was a jagged hole. She peered inside the tinted void. What she saw astonished her.

The dream was clearly disturbing. For one, there was the frog. For two, there was everything else. She told the orderly all about it. They were sitting at the breakfast table, silently spooning cereal from dull brown bowls.

Well? she said.

He looked at her with considered bemusement.

I think you're getting simpler, he said.

Sometimes at night she would wake to the sounds the mother made. The mother shouted things out in her sleep. The things she shouted were in a different language. It must have been the language of her childhood because the words she said seemed tender even though the language itself sounded harsh and spiky. At least, she assumed it was the mother. Who else could it be? One night she walked down the stairs and looked in on the mother as she slept. The mother lay there naked and curled into a ball, her back to the door. She could see the bumpy outline of the mother's spine against her pale and blotched skin. She looked like a thing that belonged in a deep, wet cave. The next night, after the mother began shouting, she sat down on the mattress next to her and began to carefully brush the mother's hair. Shhhh, she said. You are sleeping, she said. Shhhh, she said again.

After a while, she decided go back to the Chateau du Mons. She didn't really want to, but she didn't know what else to do. Certainly she couldn't stay in the house all day. Not anymore. Still, she had apprehensions. The orderly, for instance. She thought it would be weird to see the orderly at the hospital and at the house, that maybe the hospital would start to be resemble the house and the house, the hospital, or more so at least. This seemed terrible to her. Sometimes things needed to be what they were. We are held in a delicate embrace, she thought. Anything at all could mess that up.

But what if it was already messed up? She recoiled from the thought. She tried it out in her mind. She thought of the mother, the mother sitting in the darkened front room, her eyes fixed upon the flickering television, her cigarettes burning like little offerings. She thought of the mother and she went.

But at the hospital the orderly wasn't there.

He hasn't worked here in months, said the head nurse.

Lucy looked around waiting room helplessly. She thought of the orderly leaving every day, kissing her on the forehead, uttering words like a catechism. Love you, have a good day, see you later.

Are you sure? she asked.

Am I sure?! the nurse exclaimed. Let me ask you something: Do I look like I don't know the color of my own underpants?

The hospital seemed different. It was dirtier now and somehow damp. Patients shuffled around aimlessly and coughed into the air. Attendants were scarce. In fact, there didn't seem to be anyone attending anything at all. Had it always looked like this?

Maybe it's more like weeks, the nurse said, a bit more softly. He'll be back anyway. You'll see.

Then the nurse's expression changed, hardened. She looked at Lucy coolly.

They always come back, she said.

The head nurse put her in a room with a wizened woman with a round flabby face. Her name was Mrs. Taylor and the problem with Mrs. Taylor, the head nurse said, was that she wouldn't eat or take her pills. The head nurse pinched Mrs. Taylor's cheek and wiggled it. She just won't cooperate with her own care, the head nurse said, sweetly. But I think you two will be good for each other. Yes, I think, this will be the very thing.

The old woman farted loudly and stared at the window. The pills were there in a little paper cup in front of her.

Hi, she said.

Mrs. Taylor said nothing.

What should we do today? she said.

Mrs. Taylor didn't respond. She didn't even look at Lucy. She just continued her staring.

They finished the shift in silence.

Back at the house the orderly and the mother were sitting at the table. The orderly was eating soup. The mother was watching him.

She stood in the doorway until they noticed her. It took a while.

I went to the Chateau today, she said.

The Chateau! What for?

You weren't there.

At the Chateau?

They said you haven't been there in months.

He and the mother looked at each other. It was a sad and knowing look.

I told you that, he said.

No, she said. No you didn't.

I did, he said. Months ago. Remember?

He did, the mother said, approvingly. He told you this.

We were here. In the kitchen. And I told you that I had quit the hospital and got a job in real estate. Remember?

Lucy tried to remember but it was difficult to do in front of other people. She thought about the kitchen and tried to remember the kitchen and she thought about the orderly and tried to remember him too, but nothing happened. It seemed cruel to do that, to ask her to remember in front of other people. To perform memory. It seemed hurtful. There was nothing to be done. Her head was empty, empty and whirling.

Poor thing, the mother said.

My little lamb, the orderly said.

He wore a look of deep caring and sympathy, just like the mother.

At the Chateau, Mrs. Taylor still wasn't talking or taking her pills. This did not seem to be much of a problem for anyone. When Lucy filled out her forms and handed them to the head nurse, the nurse would scan them, make a clicking sound with her tongue, and then return to whatever it was that she was doing.

After a while Lucy grew bored with her duties and began to wander the hospital. She checked in on other patients. Surely, she thought, there must be better patients, patients who would respond to her prompts and advances. But the patients at the hospital were mostly the same. There was a woman who complained loudly about her gout and a woman who kept asking people if they wouldn't mind giving back her arm. There was also a woman who limped around the hospital calling after a kitty. Here, Isabel, the woman called. Here, sweet pea. Mommy wants to repay you for what you did. These were the kinds of women there were. The ones that talked, Lucy decided, were worse than the ones that didn't. Eventually she came back to the small woman and her pills and the window. Together they sat in silence until it was time to go.

But then one day Mrs. Taylor spoke.

This isn't my first time in the hospital, she said. Her voice was soft and hoarse. No, she said. Not at all. When I was younger, I used to make it a habit of visiting my sick friends in hospitals. I liked visiting these friends. It made me feel alive, she said, quickened, as they say, like I was touching something electric, but in the good way. Like when you touch something you can't stop touching. In fact, Mrs. Taylor continued, after a moment, I liked it so much that for a while it's all I did! I would go from one hospital to the next with my daisies and my chocolates and just sit in those rooms, those wonderful sterile rooms, and listen to whichever friend it was ramble on about their health and their dreams and their fears until it was time to go to the next visit, where I would do the same thing. This would go on all day and into the night. And when there weren't any friends in the hospital, a tragic but not unusual affair to be sure, I would just go to one, any old random hospital, and *make* a friend, just so I could visit. It wasn't easy, let me tell you. The business of visiting sick friends in hospitals, it's a serious one. You have to have patience, physical stamina, emotional fortitude. You have to have a willing ear. And if you're visiting people you don't yet know, well, then you have to be prepared. Often I would stand outside and listen in on other people's conversations. I'd stand outside and smoke like I was a patient or a worker and try to piece together names, so then I could go in for a visit. Or, I'd borrow a friend's dog and walk right in and tell them the therapy dog had arrived. This was more difficult, obviously. Because you have to find a place to put the dog while you visit the patients. A dog will only get in the way of a visit, you see. The whole thing becomes about the dog. *Look at the dog. What's his name? Isn't he a good little doggy?* These are the things people say when there's a dog present. You don't get anything of significance from the patient. You don't feel *wanted* with a dog in the room. So, the important thing was to find a room to stash the dog while you visited. It wasn't easy, like I said, but I had my ways. I had my ways.

Mrs. Taylor stopped for a moment to remember her ways. She looked out the window like she was peering into the porthole of a mysterious yacht. She chuckled.

Anyway, she began again, all of this was mine. The hospitals, the patients, the exhilaration of the taking of life's fading pulse. It was a grand time to be young. But then one day, as it always happens, everything changed. One day, I visited this particular sick friend. He was a young man—we were all young then of course—who but the young live this way—but this sick friend seemed to me particularly young and he had been in the hospital for so long that it seemed he had been there all his life. But even though he had been in the hospital, in and out of the hospital, you see, for so long, even though this was true, I had not yet visited him. He had called me several times to come visit, pleading to come visit, but I had ignored him. It was a busy time. I was visiting other friends, friends with diseases much more serious than his. I didn't tell him this, of course. You can't be *cruel.* Plus you never know when a mildly sick friend is going to blossom into a truly sick friend. You have to keep your options open. And sure enough, eventually my patience was rewarded and this young man, call him Frank, finally took a turn for the worse. So I borrowed an automobile and drove all the way out to the hospital where he was staying so we might, at last—what do you call it?—commune. The hospital was a mean two-story building located at the apex of a cul-de-sac, a kind of irregular, oblong cul-de-sac, an ill-designed cul-de-sac to be sure, that itself was at the end of a long industrial road, with rigorously spaced trash cans on either side. The intention of the trashcans and their spacing were unclear to me, but it seemed like as a patient you were intended to dispose of everything, strip away everything as you went, your jackets, your shoes, your hats, your caps, the soda cans in the car, the coffee cups and old newspapers, your overnight bags, even that, in order to arrive at the hospital in a state of pure anticipation. This, at least, is what I imagined. So when I walked in through the front doors of the hospital I imagined what it must feel like to have left everything behind, to come in ready. This should have been my first clue that things were about to change. This should have been my first clue to turn right around and find a usual hospital. But I was intent, you see. I was blind with desire, and I kept right on going, right through those hospital doors. Inside, the hospital felt—how can I describe it?—damp. Maybe even moist. My friend Frank was located in a small and dull orange room on the second floor, which he shared with an old woman on a ventilator. As I mentioned, this friend of mine was young and because he was young and probably for other reasons too, he held out hope that now that he was really bad off, in other words, that this thing making him sick might be killing him. But not only this! He held out further hope that the thing killing him would be singular to him. He told me all this right off the bat. He said he hoped while singular to him this thing would after it was done killing him go on to kill other people too, perhaps many people, although perhaps not in hideous ways. If he was to be honest, he said to me, he hadn't really thought about that part. While his own dying had not yet been hideous there was no telling what lay around the corner. Things that lay around corners are usually hideous and horrible, let me tell you. Lurking, that's the term for corners and their things. In any case, the point was this: the more hideous and horrible this unknown thing inside my friend, the better, he thought. Because the more hideous and horrible this thing inside him, the better chance that other people, the people who would later succumb to it, and the people around those people, and the people who merely read about sick people, would speak his name with fear and reverence. That, in the end, is what he really hoped for. To be the name of a strange and perplexing disease! What do you think of that? I'll tell you what I thought. How fantastic! That is what I thought. Just when you think you have heard everything a sick friend has to say, out comes one with something so extraordinary, he might as well have been speaking Swahili. And I remember, Mrs. Taylor said, that I wanted to capture every single word of his, to savor his unique perspective. But it was hard to concentrate in that room. First there was the sound of the ventilator stuck to the old woman's face. Whush Whush was the sound it made. Whush Whush. Plus under those horrible regulation fluorescent lights, the dull orange color took on a dream-like quality. Here he was, my friend, what's-his-name, describing how his life's ambition to be recognized was, with some good luck, finally coming true, and all I could think about was my own hands. But this, it turns out, may have been the point.

Because it seemed that at this particular hospital there were different color rooms corresponding to the patient's proximity to death. Orange was closer to death than pale yellow and yellow closer still than pink. This much I gathered on my own. I walked from room to room and snuck looks at the patients' charts. I watched as patients were transferred, fairly regularly, from one color room to another. However, no one could really explain *the purpose* for these color-coded rooms. One orderly told me about a plan implemented some time ago by the hospital administrator. He said that the idea was to correspond each disease with what the hospital administrator called its adversarial color. You see, every disease, the administrator reasoned, was said to have an essential color and each color an opposite and adversarial color, which, when applied to the area surrounding the disease would act as a tonic. So, if a patient came into the hospital complaining of kidney problems, he would be placed immediately into a green room because green is the opposite of yellow, which is the color of kidney disease. But if, once in the green room the patient's condition got worse, well then that patient would be transferred to a yellow room under the assumption that the problem was not the kidneys but instead the liver. Unless, of course, the problem was not the organ per se, but the disease attacking it, like let's say kidney stones rather than kidney failure, and so the *shade of the color,* in which case the patient, would be transferred to a room with a lighter or darker shade of yellow or green, which explained all the different colors and movements. But that, according to another orderly, was hogwash. The colors were established by a different hospital administrator, and meant as homeopathic cures, much in the manner of early treatment for madness, in which a caged red bird was placed next to a patient for a predetermined period of time in order to attract all the red sickness from the patient's body and then, having completed its task, was decapitated so that the madness died with the bird. This, according to the orderly, was the reason for all the trashcans. After a patient was better they would strip the room and burn the paint chips in the garbage cans. Oh yeah, his friend said, then why don't we never see nothing burning? It's done in the wee morning, the orderly said. Administrators don't do nothing in the wee morning, his friend replied. They don't get up before noon. Can you believe that? Burning paint? Administrators? The wee morning? What wonderful men! By this time I had lost complete track of my friend. Truthfully, the hospital had become much more interesting to me than any old sick friend. Even one who hoped to one day be a terrible disease. By the time I remembered him, he had already been discharged. Because he was better or because he was worse? I asked the discharge nurse. But she only shrugged. Who knows? is what she said. A little while later I received a note saying my sick friend had indeed died. But not of any disease, known or unknown. After he was released one day he just walked into a lake.

Mrs. Taylor stopped again. This time she looked at the wall. She sighed.

The point is: I never found out the reason for the colors, she said. For some reason, without my sick friend, the hospital was difficult to negotiate and ever more difficult to find. Every day I drove to it and you would think this would make it easier to get to, in the way that daily commuters can drive long distances and not remember a single thing about the drive or the distance and yet still arrive, right as rain, at their desired destination. But the more I drove the harder it became. At intersections, I would idle, confounded by the direction to take, horns behind me honking away, but still I would just stay there and try to think of the hospital. Think, I would say. Hospital, I would say. But the only thing this conjured up was the image of a dog in the moonlight on a neighborhood street. Sometimes I drove for five minutes and ended up back at my own home. I am becoming a loon is what I thought. This may or may not have been true. What was most certainly true was that the hospital was avoiding me. Because here was the truth of the hospital: it was a living dream. The whole point of the hospital, it finally occurred to me, was to produce that strange state I had experienced on my first visit. *This* was the reason for the colors and the lights and the ventilators and the intermittent sounds of breath and weeping. To ease the patients' passage into death. The closer you get to dying the more dreamlike everything becomes. You cease to be you in the way that you have always known, the you tied to structures like houses and jobs and people, and more and more dissolve into ideas, thoughts, and memories. You become pure. The hospital, it occurred to me, was designed to create this sensation early in an illness, to ensure the patient experiences their own most perfect self for as long as possible. The hospital was designed to be a long corridor to death!

Mrs. Taylor paused and looked triumphant. Then she looked weary. Finally she looked sad. She turned back to the window and looked outside.

It was this discovery that ultimately undid me, she said softly. Because this was also the reason why the hospital was avoiding me. Who doesn't want to live inside of a dream? Who doesn't want their mind to be the world? If word got out about such a place there is no telling what might have happened. The poor hospital would be overrun with people desperate for a somnambulant life. People like me. Of course no one believes me, the woman said. Who could? But I know it is out there. I know it is waiting. I can hear it, she said. Calling me home.

That night she told the orderly all about it. They were lying in bed trying to sleep, or he was. These days they didn't stay up late. The demands of the orderly's new job necessitated new habits. He drank vegetable juices; he did push-ups. In bed he would talk enthusiastically about the job. He would impart. The important thing, he said night after night, is belief. You have to believe. For that hour or whatever it is you believe that this house is right for this family. Maybe it is and maybe it isn't. But for the time you spend with them, no question. Sometimes I imagine I am reuniting them with a lost brother or sister they didn't even know they had. You have to pretend to be part of the family and look at the house with those eyes. Then you know what they *really* want.

It's incredible, Lucy said.

Isn't it? The orderly was lying on his stomach, head turned away from her, his hands underneath his pillow

I imagine myself in one of the yellow rooms. The dull yellow kind, as the sleep that's not yet sleep just creeps into me.

What? he said, turning onto his side and curling up his legs.

Yellow, she said. The color of transition.

What the hell are you talking about? the orderly said. He sat up and crossed his legs.

The hospital, she said. With the colors? What are you talking about?

Little lamb, little lamb, the orderly cooed. He kissed her on the forehead.

He got out of bed and walked over to a small boombox nestled in the corner of the room. In the CD drive was a disk his boss had given him. He turned it on and came back to bed.

Welcome to relaxation, a voice said. It was a deep and gentle voice that seemed like it belonged to a large bearded man.

The orderly lay down on his back and stretched out his legs. He let his arms hang loose at his sides. He stared vacantly up at the ceiling.

You are now going to relax, the voice said. But you have to choose to. It is your right to relax, but you must claim this right. We will start with your toes.

The orderly relaxed his toes. He lay next to her, silent and immobile. His chest and belly were pale, his lips bright. He still appeared delicate despite his new routines. Lucy put her hand on his chest.

Don't, he said.

Shhh, she said.

Concentrate on each toe, the voice hummed, and then concentrate on the absence of each toe. Each toe is a worry; each toe is a thought.

Behind the voice was light, spacious synthesizer music.

In thrall to the music, to the voice's assuring timber, the orderly's body was going limp and his eyes losing focus, becoming pallid, his strange and opaque eyes. She ran her hand through his hair.

I'm tired, he said.

Each toe dissolving in a pure white light.

She kissed his neck.

Trying to consolidate, he murmured. Early morning.

She sighed and lay down next to him, turning away, toward the box and its voice, the window, the intermittent sounds of other life.

Now, think of your left foot, the voice said.

Lucy thought about her left foot. She saw her left foot and saw it dissolve into light. But then she couldn't be sure if she had actually seen her left foot and not her right. Then she couldn't be sure if imagining the foot without imaging the toes was a good idea.

By now the voice was talking about her abdomen.

Your abdomen holds all your fears and dreams, it intoned.

Can we start over? she whispered. But the orderly didn't answer. She propped herself up on her elbow to look at him. His face was slack and serene; his eyes shut. She leaned down and kissed him on the lips. He didn't move. She kissed him again, pushing her tongue slightly into his mouth. He still didn't move. She chewed on his earlobe and brushed her fingertips over his hairs on his stomach. Nothing.

Your abdomen is now relaxed, the voice said. Now we must move into deeper places. Now we will begin the true unbinding.

Lucy stopped listening. Instead, she thought about the yellow room. She thought about walking into it and lying down on the unused bed. The room was quiet but outside of it there was movement. She could hear things. What were the things she heard?

Rustling things. She wanted to look but she couldn't look. Once she was on the bed, she could only be on the bed. The door to the room was open and the hall was empty. Once she had been in the hall but that was a long time ago. She lay there listening. There was an empty spot on the bed next to her.

In the middle of the night she awoke to the sound of voices. On the tape the bearded man was still speaking. This time, however, there was no music at all. It was just his calm assured voice.

I love you, the bearded man was saying. And I will always love you. Let my voice caress you in your darkest most unwitting hours.

The orderly was curled up into a ball. His mouth formed a slight smile.

You are worthy of this love, said the bearded man. Your hair is voluptuous and gets stronger every day. You are vigorous and full-blooded. Nothing can stop the confident flow of your blood.

But his wasn't the only voice. Far away there were also voices. Lucy slipped out of bed and into the hall. It was dark in the hall, as it had been in the room, much darker than usual. There was no light from the outside, no moonlight, no lamplight, and the air around her felt viscous. Around and beneath her it seemed like almost visible things were moving.

They brushed past her with gentle purpose. She stopped at the stairs and listened but she couldn't hear anything.

The next day, Lucy came to work eager to continue where she and Mrs. Taylor had left off. She was excited. The hospital, it seemed to her, Mrs. Taylor's hospital, was an unexpected gift, something improbable slipped into her hand almost casually—a mash note, a locked wooden jewelry box, a tiny porcelain doll with glass animal eyes—something whose very existence changed the landscape around her, reoriented her, so that she felt suddenly like one of those heroes in the stories her brother used to read to her, alone together in his darkened room, his voice low, his eyes bright, those heroes whose success on their journeys necessitated the intervention of a wise woman or talking bird, handing over necessary objects, items taken on faith at first—an tincture of oil, a crust of bread—but whose purpose, at the right time—on the treacherous mountain path, sky darkened and whirling, in front of the howling, hungry dog—became brilliantly clear, the whole quest now merely a series of moves, of feints—he squeezed her hand, he licked his lips—and she could feel it, this sudden understanding, pressing on her shoulders, her hips, she could see beyond the ridge, the pass—she could see the opening and the glittering kingdom and she knew what she had to do.

Hello, she said as she entered the room, smiling. What do you want to talk about today?

Mrs. Taylor looked at her without recognition.

Maybe you could tell me another story, she said. About another sick friend?

Mrs. Taylor turned her head and looked out the window.

Or you could just tell me the same story, Lucy said. This isn't your first time in the hospital, she began encouragingly.

But the woman didn't respond. Next to her on a tray a small Dixie cup contained two multicolored pills. In front of her, out the window, there was only this: some brown grass and in the distance some houses, small houses, and the sky of relentless blue.

Meanwhile, back at the house the mother had decided to move into the room down the hall from their room. Or rather the orderly decided it for her. There were eight other rooms in the house, but this was the one for her. What if something happened? the orderly reasoned. There is no way they could hear her on the first or second floor. Plus it would be cozy, all of them living in close quarters like that. It would be like a proper family.

Ok, said Lucy.

Ok? the orderly asked. He seemed genuinely surprised.

It's ok, she said.

The mother was getting worse. This much was clear. When Lucy woke in the middle of the night sometimes she found the mother was at the kitchen table, smoking cigarettes and staring at the stove. Other times she wasn't in the house at all. The door would be open, wide open, to the desolate nocturnal street. For a while she would stand in the doorway and softly call out the mother's name. Then she would close the door, leave it unlocked and return to bed. In the morning the door would be locked and the mother would be asleep on the couch. One night, though, she followed the mother out into the street. She waited until there would be enough of a distance between them. Through the window she watched the mother walk about the door and into the front yard. The yard was defined by high hedges and a trellis entryway. Where there should have been grass there were indiscriminate thickets and patches of indecently large coneflowers. When the girls had lived here the yard had been tended. Almost every day there was something new planted in the yard. Since then it had become overgrown and unmanageable. It didn't even occur to Lucy that she should do something about it. Now looking at it, she couldn't tell if this was because she didn't care or because she did. She waited until the mother passed through the trellis. But when she got to the street the mother was gone. Where did she go? The houses around her offered nothing. Standing there, Lucy could still smell the mother's perfume, which was blunt and synthetically floral. When she returned to the house, the orderly was in the hallway with the mother. Both looked like they had been suddenly awakened by a frightful alarm. What are you doing? the orderly asked her. Yes, the mother agreed. What *was* she doing?

In her room the orderly beamed at her. He turned to leave but stopped at the door and came back

Are you sure? he asked.

Sure? she said.

Sure, he said.

Yeah, she said.

He turned to leave again and then stopped again and came back again.

What is all this? he asked her.

She was sitting on the floor surrounded by maps. They were maps of the city and its surrounding areas, current maps and older maps, their edges overlapping, a tumult of thin lines and pastel geometry. Some areas had been circled in red ink.

This? she said and looked at him looking at her. His lips were thin. But a slight scar gave them character. She remembered thinking this. She remembered when she had attended his mouth like that, when, in the darkness of the deep morning, he would begin rub his hands on her and then they would sit and smoke cigarettes at the rusty metal table in the backyard, when every word from that mouth, and her mouth too, opened a new door, betrayed a new corridor.

It's nothing, she said.

It was after the mother had moved into the room upstairs and after she had started her map that her own mother began calling. The woman who had been her mother. Once.

The phone would ring and Lucy would answer it and her mother would already be in the middle of a sentence about the importance of windows or how she kept losing this one red shoe. At least it seemed like these were the things she was talking about. It was difficult to tell exactly. Hello? she would say. Mom? But her mother never responded. Instead she continued to ramble on for a while and then hung up. It was like she was listening in on the conversation. Like someone had arranged for Lucy to hear her mother talk to strangers.

But she left messages too. Her mother. And the messages were as odd as the phone calls, but they were different because they implicated her directly. You should be more careful, one message said. I had thought we raised you to be careful. I was talking to your father today, another said. And we both agreed that, if we were to do it over again, we would have read you entirely different bedtime stories. There is something perverse about all that magic and going places.

One day her mother left one that said, For years I've dreamt that you were a tiny grey bird I held cupped in my hands, through which I could, without intention, feel the fluttering of your heart and the hollow fragility of your bones. I knew that at any moment I would close my hands and crush you, a feeling less apprehensive than relieving in its certainty.

Then there was a sound and for a moment her mother was distracted. Come home darling, we miss you.

She called her mother back.

You have to stop calling me, she said.

Things are different now, she said.

What the hell are you talking about, her mother said.

Usually when the calls came she walked to the empty room at the end of the hall. What had once been the empty room. Now it was the mother's room. And the mother was always there. She was there and she wanted things. Before she didn't seem to want anything. Before it was cigarettes and tea and the television in the darkened circular room, but now all she did was want. Things in this case mostly meant foodstuffs and knickknacks. She called out for them. She called them by name. Herring, she said, pinwheel. Ice cream, she said, bonnet. There was no end to the mother's appetites. But when Lucy found these things, even when she *could* find them, these necessities, these totems, even when she found them and brought them to the mother, the mother did not want them. They were not right. It was a different brand of herring, a different kind of ice cream, what is this, a teddy the bear? This is no teddy the bear! What kind of bear is wearing coats! No, the mother said. No, no, no. She threw the teddy bear against the wall. It was dark in the room and the mother's breathing was strained. The teddy bear slumped against the wall. It had black button eyes and wore galoshes along with the offending raincoat. The mother's hand grasped Lucy's wrist. It was bony and dry and strong. The hand. Sometimes at night, when the mother cried out and shivered and Lucy came to her and whispered things and brushed her hair, the mother's wrists, her hands, felt fragile as they fussed and clawed at the invisible torments around her. They felt like dry and delicate nests. But now it was dark and the room littered with discarded objects, it was not that mother. It was a different mother. The mother fixed her in her cold stare. She said: A thing is not always a thing. Her voice was soft but strong, and hoarse.

Y es, the mother *was* getting worse.

Lucy walked down the hall to her own room, which more and more resembled the mother's. For one thing there was stuff everywhere. The maps of the city were scattered all over the floor and her clothes were piled, here and there, on top of the maps or just on the floor. In a corner some dirty plates and bowls remained stacked. Even the walls seemed kind of stained. She picked through the mess, gathering the maps together, and sat on the bed to look at them. The bed was a lumpy mattress on a box spring on the floor. When he had moved in, the orderly had wanted to get them a real bed, one with a frame and a headboard. It was important, he argued, though she couldn't remember why. And they had tried it, getting the frame, the headboard, the whole thing, the bed off the ground, levitating, almost. But she couldn't sleep like that. Who could sleep like that?

She got up and turned on the radio. Outside her window was a big institutional building that used to be a factory of some sort. For a while it had been empty. Now a bunch of boys lived there. It was hard to tell how many exactly. People came and went like stray cats. Today one of them was sunning himself on the roof, even though there wasn't much sun. He wore jean shorts without a shirt or shoes. His skin looked pale and tight.

On the radio, a young man with a high-pitched voice was talking about fraught but necessary journeys. He said: The Underworld is a place of power and beauty. It's a primeval place. But getting there isn't easy. You gotta activate your own essential deathliness. You gotta endeavor toward stillness. It's not so simple, ok? It's not a walk in the park. But it *is* important. Because it's in the Underworld that you will encounter your power animal. And you power animal is your one true friend.

Lucy sat back down on the bed and concentrated on the maps. The hospital, it seemed, did move. On a map from thirty years ago, a hospital that looked like the hospital as the old woman had described it—the long entry road, the cul-de-sac—occupied a place on the outskirts of the city to the south. However, on a map from only ten years later, the place where the hospital had been was now a development, and the hospital had moved across town to the north side of the city. Ten years after that it had moved farther out from the city to the surrounding areas, expanses of grass fields and occasional small forests, and now it was on the west side. Recent maps disclosed nothing at all. She looked for it everywhere but nothing resembling the hospital could be found. It was like the hospital had used itself up, like the very idea of it was no longer necessary and so it had simply just disappeared out of neglect. But this, she knew, couldn't possibly be true.

Only your power animal can lead you back to the Middle World, the young man was saying, which is, you know, the goal of all true beings. Your power animal is your friend, he said, make no mistake. But you have to discover him. You must actively seek him out. And this will mean travel. It will mean questing through the landscapes of the Underworld. You have be careful, though. Many other things can come to you in the guise of your animal. Many things are seeking entry without the necessary gift.

From the other end the hall the mother made a sound that was a little like coughing and little like moaning. She stopped for a moment. Then she made it again. This time it was louder.

On the radio show someone had called in to talk about his problems with the Underworld. Look, the caller was saying, I went questing. I went on my goddamn quest. I stayed in a cave for three days. It was dark in that cave. It was wet. You know how I know this was my place? For exactly those goddamned reason. Because it was a dank fucking hole. That's how I knew. And so I stayed there and meditated and embraced the goddamned spirit world. And you know what appeared at the end of my quest? You know what arrived to lead me home? A pigeon. A goddamn pigeon. The rats of the motherfucking sky.

The mother made the sound again and then there was sound of something crashing and then there was silence.

Seriously!? the caller on the radio shouted into the ether. I could have stayed right here and been found by a fucking pigeon! I didn't need a vision quest to come to that relentless truth.

She got up and walked back down the hall to the mother's room, where it was still quiet but now instead the mother making was clawing motions at the air in front of her and turning her head from side to side.

She sat down on the bed. There, there, she said, putting her hand on the mother's forehead. The skin was slack and cold and sweaty.

No, the mother said.

It's ok, she said.

I'm tired, the mother said.

Then you should sleep, she said.

No sleep, the mother said. No.

Sleep is your friend, she said. Sleep will help.

You are trying to kill me, the mother said, matter-of-factly.

Lucy sighed and stroked the mother's hair, which was matted and greasy. The mother batted her hand away and muttered something under her breath, which smelled like decay.

It's ok, she said.

The mother didn't respond. But her face contorted and eyes became glossy and it looked like she was going to cry, like any minute, she would just exorcise her soggy, insistent demons. But she didn't cry. Her face just stayed that way, contorted and grotesque, a hideous mask, a reflective surface. Her face stayed like that—pleading. She crawled over the mother and got in bed beside her. It smelled putrid—astringent and festering. She lay next to the mother and tried to think of the hospital, about how if she were the hospital where she would go next. The mother exhaled deeply and relaxed a little. Sleep was not her friend. Sleep would not help. But it would calm her for a little while. At least there was that.

From her room down the hall, the voice on the radio intoned. It was distant and muted, but still audible; echoing, murmuring, it made its errant way toward her, crawling, cajoling, and speaking of trees. The trees were tall. The trees were old. They were so tall that you could not see the tops, could not see the sky, the canopy was so dense, the night sky, which was dark, though dotted dimly with stars, a smearing of stars, that if you were to see them, if you could only see them, clumped together and promising patterns, would surely help you find your way. But here on the forest floor, there was no light. It was only this darkness, this different darkness, this embracing and suffocating darkness, plus the whispering. The forest floor was soft and spongy. Underneath her feet, twigs cracked. Underbrush—it must be underbrush—grabbed at her, pulled at her, desired her wholly. Somewhere there was a house. A little house with a light on and a table set for two. This is where she was going. A little house, a table, a candle and a wish. In the darkness close by, she heard the sounds of birds and other animals. They too wanted her, wanted her for something undefined yet dire. But she was not afraid. She had walked through other woods, through deeper darker and more haunted woods. She heard them and knew them, but she was not afraid.

But were they laughing? The trees. Were they laughing? No, it wasn't the trees. It was people. People were laughing. She woke up and people were laughing. It was coming from outside.

Beside her, the bed was empty. Where the mother had been was now a tangle of sheets and blankets.

The laughing came in erratic bursts. A voice shrieked and another voice giggled and there was also music, which pulsed faintly in a low register.

She got up and looked around the room. It was dark and shapes of ambiguous intent loomed in the corners. She looked out the window. The boys and a bunch of their friends were on top of the roof having a party. Different-colored paper lanterns hung from metal poles. People congregated in small groups to talk and laugh and brush up against each other. In the middle of the roof two boys and a girl danced with each other in slow, haphazard movements.

She walked down the hall. The mother was on the bathroom floor. She was naked and curled around the toilet and the acrid smell of urine wafted off the body. Lucy could see a thin skein of liquid pooled around the mother's pelvis and running into the grout. Shit, she thought.

She squatted down beside the body and shook it, gently. Hey, she said, softly. Hey.

The mother didn't respond. But the body wasn't cold; it wasn't still. The mother's shoulders rose slightly under the slow engine of breath. The mother would remain.

She got up and went back to the mother's room to get a pillow. Once she had wanted to live in this room. When she had first arrived at the house, the room was empty. It had belonged to a girl who had left and promised to come back but had never returned. The girl had left all of her things and sometimes one of the other girls would come in and clean and arrange everything to make it ready just in case the girl returned that very day. She would sit on the bed and stare at the clothes and imagine that she was that girl that had left and come back. Or maybe she was about to leave and would never come back. She might have been someone like that, someone desired, whose memory would be tended with care and devotion, like some forgotten saint whose impenetrable mountain shrine only the most zealous of acolytes, robed in black and softly chanting while they stumbled and clawed their way through barbed crags and detrital slopes to the damp and holy grotto, could attain.

Outside the boys and their friends conducted their social rituals with abandon. Down the hall the mother waited.

The mother waited, yes. Always waiting, yes. And Mrs. Taylor and the orderly and her own mother too—her own mother, there at the kitchen table, once, eyes on the window, its pallid light a judgment, whispering something—a prayer? a wish?—*one more for the reliquary,* and holding in her hands a cardboard cigar box filled with baseball cards, a smiling king painted on it.

Or him, eyes marbles, lips licked, saying, I will never leave—his voice soft and hoarse—I will never leave—when she had come to him, had ridden through the dunes to the highway and along the shoulder there, trucks passing, roaring and the trees that whispered and pressed, the woods, as she pedaled and pedaled until it was dark and the man with a green Impala stopped and said, *what in God's name are you doing out here?*

That's not a penguin, he said. The brother. This was in his room watching TV, which was small, the room, and without windows, but also the TV too, and there was another bed there, where Larry slept. That's Larry's bed, he said, scratching and scratching, but absently, his fingernails dull, his forearm, red trails there. As if she already knew who that was.

Larry. She thought of a man with a moustache and dull hair. A man wiping his nose on his sleeve. They sat on his bed; they sat next to each other but it was so small, the bed. Too small. On the TV a giant fish ate smaller fish—long and scaly it dove into the panicked schools. Too small. Enough for only one. A capsule, a coffin, not a boat to distant lands.

But it wasn't really him, was it?

For example, he didn't say: To think right you have to hold your head like this. Or: I am the terrible king of the swamp and right now only my memory. Or: You are my deepest and loveliest secret, one I will never give up. He said: we're not allowed, is what he said. When she put his arm around his waist, he said it, and stared at her like a fish stares, eyes marbles, or a doll—see?—so they sat together in the room without windows not talking and imagining and what would happen if they were talking and then it was time to go because a large woman stood in the doorway and said it was.

There's only one exit and it is waiting in the shallows.

On the ride back, she realized it must be an act. Or a code. Something. Because it wasn't really him, was it? And the man in the green Impala put her bike in the trunk and buckled her in and his hands were big and smooth. Like if she took every third word it would say: *It is just another game. It is just another game. It is just another game. Find me.* But the Impala man's hands were big and smooth and he kept talking, saying, those are pretty earrings and what does your father think of your earrings and what does it feel like when your mother scolds you? So that she couldn't remember, not exactly, the words, even when, later, she wrote them down, everything, or tried to, alone in her room, the voices beneath her.

And her father said: Do you have something to say to your mother?

And her mother said: A thing with fangs is a good thing to be.

And the doctors said: What do you think about when I say the word "tree"?

And everything is always waiting, waiting but not knowing. Because who really waits? Who feels it, the readiness and the hole? She took the scissors and cut. Refashioning, refashioning. Because in the hospital there is no waiting, only the floating and the endless dream. Because the hospital is like a big dog that takes you up on its back and nestles you into its downy fur, which is soft but also buoyant, like you're suspended there, in the fur, thick and caressing, like a fog and you can think, hey dog, take me to Madagascar and the dog will go there and show you its wonders, and you could say, hey dog I want an ice cream soda and he would find you the best ice cream soda, one you can eat for hours and hours without end, because that's his job, the dog, the dog that is a hospital, that's its job—to make your thoughts find endings always.

And it was only much later that she understood that what he was actually saying, the brother—even after she went back and asked and heard the nurse say: well there's no one here by *that* name—that what he was saying—sitting in the windowless room, his voice low and hoarse—was home, home, home.

So she finished the map and took it to the Chateau. She and Mrs. Taylor would figure this out. They would sit down and find out where it would appear next. Because the hospital was meant for people like them. For her, for Mrs. Taylor. Yes it was skittish. Yes it was shy. But that just meant you had to approach it with an open hand. You had to whisper while you went.

She showed the map to Mrs. Taylor and together they studied its contours.

There are three possible places the hospital could be, she said.

Mrs. Taylor looked at her with kind eyes and smiled.

We're at the hospital, dear, she said.

No, said Lucy, lowering her voice a little bit. Not this hospital. *Your* hospital.

Mrs. Taylor looked at the map again. It was actually several maps that had been cut up and pasted together. This seemed to confuse the woman. She looked at the paper and touched it lightly, brushing her fingers over its various and multicolored shapes, over its plates and rifts.

I remember going to a ball once, Mrs. Taylor, brightly. A masquerade where everyone was dressed like a cat.

She frowned for a moment.

Do cats have stripes or do they have spots? Mrs. Taylor said. Because everyone had spots but they also had whiskers.

Concentrate, Lucy said. Here are the places. Here, here, and here.

She pointed again to the map.

We're a long way from there, Mrs. Taylor said, helpfully, and patted her hand.

Lucy looked at her, blissful and vacant, staring at a painting of a group of happy cherubs having tea.

We don't have to be, she said, at last.

Oh, said Mrs. Taylor, that's nice.

As she was leaving the head nurse stopped Lucy in the hall.

I know what you are doing, the head nurse said.

I'm not doing anything, she said.

Let's talk about it, said the head nurse.

They took the head nurse's car to a coffee shop several blocks away.

Inside the car was one white jogging shoe, a pair of binoculars, and a copy of magazine called UNCAGED that boasted an inside look at the lives of your favorite fighters and displayed a angry, square-faced man glaring from the cover. It smelled like synthetic pine.

Of course we could have walked the head nurse said as they navigated out of the parking lot and onto the street. But then we would have missed out on all this wonderful alone time.

Across the street from the coffee shop was a man with no hands asking for money. He sat against the large brick wall of a bank and held up a sign with his handless wrists. The sign said: I am not without my vanities. With him was a small, brown dog.

They sat at a table next to the shop's large picture window. Outside, people walked past the man with no hands, flattering themselves secretly as they went. Meanwhile, he scolded his dog, who ignored him and seemed to be eyeing something unseen by the way it pulled and thumped its tail against the cement.

You know what's good? the head nurse said. Coffee with honey.

She took a sip of her coffee.

Honey is a great cure-all, the head nurse said. It's famous for its medicinal properties as well as its religious significance. Did you know that Hippocrates, the father of all medicine, lived in a sepulchre with a swarm of bees? It's reported that they advised him on all matters diagnostic. Of course, such things are probably not entirely factual. But to think of them in such ways is, in the end, to miss the point. Don't you think?

She took another sip.

Mmmm, she said.

Inside the shop, someone's idea of soothing music played. An older woman dressed in a baggy grey business suit read a book with a woman riding a bear on the cover and laughed to herself as she wrote things in a leather-bound notebook.

Lucy took a sip of her own coffee. It was bitter, almost burnt, and her mouth and stomach rioted against it.

Of course, the head nurse said. It's not always so simple. Take the coffee you're drinking right now. Is it good for you? Bad for you? The reports are contradictory. What we know is an unfolding spiral. Would you like to try it with honey?

Lucy shook her head.

Your loss, the head nurse said.

At a nearby table a man in a goatee was counseling a fidgety woman. Figure out your brand and be the brand, he said. Be. The. Brand.

Let me tell you a story, the head nurse said. And then she did.

It was a story about a mother and a child. Therefore it was a story about love. In the story, the mother loved the child very much and they would do everything together. They went to the park and fed the ducks; they climbed onto jungle gyms; they sat in the middle of their living room and had elaborate pretend dinner parties; they even slept in the same bed and, it seemed to them, or at least the mother, dreamed the same dreams. But even so, the mother was never sure her daughter loved her. How can anyone know such a thing? Children are, in the end, mysteries. And this child, her daughter, was more mysterious than most. She was particularly independent. She created worlds for herself and lived there, far from the mother's grasp. She was solitary and often solemn. In fact, from the child's very first moment, the mother later said, she could tell there was something unreachable in her. The mother felt this unreachable thing growing in her daughter every single day, metastasizing. So this mother did what any mother would do in such circumstances. She mustered all her love and instinct and took drastic action. She began to fake her own death. This was years later, after the child had grown some and even more away from her. What she would do is this: in the afternoon, after cleaning the house meticulously—details were important—the mother would take sleeping pills and lie down on her bed. Before doing this she would place a short note she had written upon the dresser. The note did not say goodbye; it did not make declarations of love and support. The note simply and lovingly described a memory, a memory of the two of them together, of a time when the child was younger and they were, to the mother's mind, closer and therefore happier. These memories were bathed in sunlight, muted, hazy, and somehow warmer than real sunlight. The mother wrote them down carefully, then took the pills, and stared at the ceiling, where a crack ran from the corner to something near the center. The next thing she always remembered was the child shaking her violently from sleep, a frenzy of movement, and most importantly the look on the child's face—one of absolute devotion, though maybe also panic and need. Then the mother felt loved. She felt truly and for the first time in a long time the force of her child's touch. She held onto this love; she caressed it in her memories, this face and its desperation, sometimes for a week, sometimes a month. It sustained her. Eventually, though, she would need to go back to the well and replenish herself.

This went on for a year, maybe two. And, as often happens, the two of them settled into a routine. In some part of her, the daughter always knew what to expect from what she called the event and so her own reactions became more muted. Still though there was underneath it all genuine fear, genuine need, and this still came across, even through the growing bitterness and exasperations. Enough at least for the mother. But in truth the mother began to care less and less about this aspect of the so-called event, about the daughter and the daughter's reaction. She needed it less. More important were the memories and the long sleeping. Often now at nights she wrote a memory in secret, wrote only for herself, then read it, tore it up, took some pills (now she needed more), and drifted off to sleep. There she found in her dream life a place that was like the memories but not the memories. She found a place created by the memories and dictated by their logic, but with more autonomy of movement and expression. In other words, she found a home. Once she told her daughter in the middle of a fight about money, "In my dreams when I am with you, you are four. This to me is your perfect age." This was the beginning of the end. The daughter could not stand to go unseen like that, or rather to be seen but to be seen wrongly, to not be seen for her true self, which was clearly the person she was right then, right at that moment. After all the mother had put her through, for her to diminish her like that, it seemed unfair. Eventually she packed up her stuff and moved in with a boyfriend, who, as these things happen, became a string of boyfriends, each one resembling the last. The mother, on the other hand, though saddened by the departure, was, for a while, content with her dreaming, if content was the right word. Day and night she dreamed. In her dreams the mother and daughter lived together in a small house that was like their house but it was clean and bright. Sometimes it was in the clearing of a tangled wood and other times it was on a sunny neighborhood block, where all the houses looked like the small house. She could never remember what they did in the house. But it was enough that she could remember her daughter and the house together. It was enough. However eventually, of course, it was not enough. For soon she could no longer remember the dreams, could not ever remember the feelings they produced. She woke every time. The increasing amounts of sleeping pills she took had sabotaged her memory as well as leaving her with lung and bladder problems. She ended up dying alone and in pain, navigating the endless, cold vacuum of her dreamless sleep. The daughter, on the other hand became a respected professional in a necessary field. She had a daughter of her own. She prospered. The head nurse finished and took a triumphant sip from her coffee cup.

The point here, the head nurse elaborated, is that, generally speaking, you can either be the daughter or you can be the mother. You can look at any given situation with the light of clarity or you can pretend that tenderness means love. The Mrs. Taylors of the world, they're just pills, memories, tonics. They're alluring, sure. They do the job for a little while. But in the end they leave you adrift. But you, you have the gift, the head nurse told her. You have reserves. I see you: always circling, circling, circling the wound. The endless night, that's your métier. Poor wounded thing! That's what people say, I bet. Poor little lamb. But they don't understand you, yes? They don't see how are a magnet for it all. How much you want it, the wound, the tongue, the endless night. How everything you do is a chance to be close to it all again. That's what I'm offering. A chance, an arena, a happy home. You are capable of the kinds of things this line of work entails. This noble calling. This respected profession in a necessary field. Think it over. I have high hopes for you. I really do.

That night she took Mrs. Taylor and went out in search of the hospital. Her hospital. Theirs.

She came back to the Chateau as evening emerged and put Mrs. Taylor in the hospital van and together they drove toward the dark, headlong. It wasn't hard to do. The head nurse was at home with her cat, Murphy, feeding it canned sardines while on the television a man in a trench coat was telling a puffy-faced woman there would be no escape. And at the Chateau the night nurse was flirting with Oscar the orderly, who was saying, no, no, you gotta hold it in for a while, let it really grab your insides. So she fished the keys from the front desk's drawer and said to Mrs. Taylor, now is the time, and Mrs. Taylor looked at her, opened her mouth, but didn't say anything.

They drove down the hill and out past the water treatment plant and the desolate mall, which but for a sordid deli and a small place selling socks had now shed most of its shops, until, for a while, it was only dimly held developments, and the night. Lucy tuned the dial low and found a station where the music hissed and thrummed and they could be at peace. The only lights were the street lights, pale and insistent.

The first possibility turned out to be merely an empty lot; the second a seminary. A hospital? a sleepy novice said, licking chapped lips, who do you think we are? Franciscans? He laughed a brittle laugh. The lot, a scrum of weeds and bottles. The seminary, one of dreams.

So they circled back again, around the city, to get to the final spot, the final possibility. She had saved this one for last because it held the most promise, she felt. Sometimes people can only go so far, she told the orderly, or would have. Was telling him. Sometimes they have find the place to sink. But he only smiled his pleasuring smile.

Suddenly Mrs. Taylor uttered a low moan and then spoke. Oblong tincture potato, she said but wasn't surprised at her words.

Lucy looked at her through the rearview mirror. There was no getting around it: Mrs. Taylor was also getting worse. For the past week she had been withholding the woman's pills in hopes of inducing in her the clarity that had first brought the dream hospital to light. But when she brought it up, the hospital, when she asked point blank: I need you to tell me about the hospital with the yellow rooms, Mrs. Taylor always talked about other things. She looked up to the ceiling as if she was waiting for something, some sign. But one time she told her a long story about her husband getting bit by a wombat on a trip to Australia. Her husband, she had said, Ralph, she said, a name she had never liked and which was in fact actually repulsive to her, so repulsive that she could never say it out loud or whisper it or even think it, not even on their wedding day, and would only call him both to his face and in her own mind by pet names like Honey Bear, Mr. Handsome, or Tootles, which was the name she used on her wedding day, Tootles. And she had tried, she said, how she had tried, to get him to change it to something better, Vespasian for example, who had been a very successful emperor even though he was as short man, like Tootles himself, but importantly not too successful, not dominant like, for example, his successor Trajan, who once fought a lion in the Colosseum and who extended the empire to its greatest reach and power, and who was so revered he had been deified in the midst of his dying rather than posthumously, because you have to be practical when it comes to new names. You can't just shoot the moon and hope character wins the day. Names are destiny and come with responsibility. Like yours, dear, she said and patted Lucy's hand.

But that was the last coherent thing Mrs. Taylor had said. After that it was the thing about cats and masquerades and now, now when Lucy needed her the most, there was just this moaning or uttering words that made no sense. It had been happening since yesterday.

She exited the highway onto a frontage road and as they got closer Mrs. Taylor began to shift in her wheel chair. She moved like there was something underneath her skin.

Are we there? Lucy asked her. Can you feel it?

Opossum liberty talcum powder, Mrs. Taylor said.

And the way she said it seemed forceful and calm. Like she was saying yes or turn right or go slowly, we must take all necessary precautions.

They turned onto a road that was a long industrial road. There weren't any trash cans but there were places on the ground where trash cans once might have been. Places where the ground was slightly disturbed and those places were, it seemed to her, they must be rigorously spaced.

Lucy stood in front of one of the demarcations, a kind of half circle, in the full halo of the van's blinding headlights. Beyond her things were moving in the dark, travelling with intention, with care. She returned to the van and took out a duffle bag with Mrs. Taylor's things. An esoteric grouping. A picture of a younger Mrs. Taylor, mid 50s, surrounded by tanned and shirtless men giving the camera the thumbs up. A cracked yellow tea cup from Portugal painted with somber shepherds. Her dresses, her skirts, her sparkling tops—none of which she wore any longer. And a faux pearl necklace she would sometimes wear to dinner on Sundays. Lucy put them in the dusty half circle, dropping each item as if discarding refuse. Then from her pocket she took out her grandfather's pocket watch. Dark and golden, it shone in the headlights. On the inside of its case words were inscribed. To Molly: Everything is Biding, it said. They had never seemed right to her, those words. She placed it there too.

And at the end of the road was the cul-de-sac and at what must be the apex of the cul-de-sac, yes, yes, was a building and that building, though, was dark.

Or mostly it was dark. Underneath the jagged black portico, beyond the glass doors, a fluorescent light was on.

C'mon, she said, and maneuvered Mrs. Taylor, who groaned a little and muttered something, out of the van and pushed her to the entrance where the electric door still, after some time standing, waiting, stamping, and waving, worked.

They were about to embark on a last great adventure. To disappear into the gauzy present. And once, she thought, there was a boy who disappeared.

They stood there in front of it, two blinking acolytes, as the door opened and closed, opened and closed, opened and closed.

But inside the hospital there was no one and nothing. There were long hallways that turned into short hallways that turned back into long hallways. The hallways, rooms and closets filled with scattered files and junked equipment. For a while they wandered the vestibule, the halls, inspecting each room. There had to be a something, a portent, a sign. She wheeled Mrs. Taylor around like a dowsing rod. Somewhere they would find it. And when they passed the elevator, the woman exhaled, so Lucy pressed the button. Going up.

They got off on the second floor and Lucy heard voices. Muted, reverberating—she couldn't tell what they were saying.

She pushed Mrs. Taylor cautiously in the sound's direction.

In the hall around a corner, sitting slumped against the aqua brick, surrounded by even more papers and folders, a boy and a girl, teenage twins. At least, she *thought* they were twins. They looked like twins. They were deep in consultation, the boy holding the girl's forearm, white and speckled, head bent close to it, peering and saying, without more testing there's really no way to know.

The girl said, But the test itself, it's just so hard on my system. On everything.

She looked stricken, exhausted.

It's the bind we're in, he said and frowned.

Oh wow, the boy exclaimed, turning his head to notice Lucy and Mrs. Taylor, look at that.

I'm trying, said the girl, her expression changing quickly to one of curiosity, excitement. But I'm not sure what I see. What do you think?

That's the problem with eyes, said the boy. If only we had fly eyes. Segmented. Multitudinous. Godlike. Then...

Then what?

The boy considered it.

I don't know, he said. But something interesting. Don't you think?

He licked his lips and swallowed, turned his attention back to Lucy and Mrs. Taylor.

Hello! he said.

Come closer, the girl said.

New and radiant friends.

We won't bite.

Or kick.

You kick. In your sleep you kick.

But *only* in my sleep.

That doesn't make it right.

Sleep, the boy said, is a confessional. You can't be blamed for what you do in your sleep.

That depends on who you're sleeping with, said the girl.

She smiled and the boy lifted a delicate, pale hand and gathered up her hair into a bun, pulling it tight, too tight. The girl's face hardened for a moment.

You're prettier this way, he said.

Lucy looked at the twins who looked back at Lucy and Mrs. Taylor. Mrs. Taylor looked at the floor, breathing a raspy breath. The boy squeezed the girl's hand.

Speak, the boy said, finally, with flourish, to Lucy. Whatever you are: we are bound to hear.

What could she do?

We didn't mean to, she said to Mrs. Taylor, herself, disturb you or anything…

The boy and girl looked at each other, knowingly.

We should go, she said

Lucy pulled Mrs. Taylor backwards a little bit.

No, the girl said. You can't go! You just got here!

They both scrambled to stand up, the boy leaping to his feet and bounding over, the girl slipping on a file and falling back down onto her behind. She looked stunned for a moment, then she began to cry.

The boy turned to look at her and then at Lucy and then back at her and then again at Lucy. He licked his lips and swallowed. Then he walked over to Lucy and, pressing his palm against the cool aqua brick, leaned there, affecting nonchalance.

Listen, he said. Don't freak out. It's cool. See? Everything is cool. You're obviously here for a reason. We all are. Here of all places. The great waiting room. We come all the time. Right? We know what it's like. We've been here forever. I think we can help you. You're here for a reason. Just tell us what it is and we'll work it out.

I'm better now, THANK YOU, the girl said, sniffling loudly.

She's fabulous, by the way, the boy said, reaching out to stroke Mrs. Taylor's cheek.

I'm ABSOLUTELY FINE, the girl said.

Lucy began to pull the wheelchair away, but under the boy's touch, his caress, Mrs. Taylor closed her eyes and slumped into the chair a little, relaxed.

See, he said. Look. All good. All good. Your friend here knows the truth of it.

He smiled. His teeth were greyish.

Lucy looked at the boy in front of her, expectant, and the girl, legs splayed on the floor, pouting. There was something familiar about them.

I'm Kent. That's Kitty. See. We're all friends now, K? What's a little secret between friends, right?

Once there was a boy who disappeared and he left a girl behind. He left a girl alone. So what, in the end, could she really do?

They've come for us, said Kitty, over her shoulder—she was on her hands and knees, crawling, her face close to the floor, crawling, looking for something among all the papers and folders—to us. It's like Christmas! The next phase.

Don't mind Kitty.

Always mind Kitty, said Kitty, fussing among the papers. She needs everything she can get.

Kent was still stroking Mrs. Taylor and Mrs. Taylor nuzzled it, his gentle hand.

We're looking, said Lucy.

Obviously.

For a hospital.

You're in luck!

We should go, Lucy said again. I made a mistake.

No, no, please. I'm sorry. We haven't had guests in so long. It's only just us.

Got it! Kitty exclaimed holding up a file.

Lucy pulled Mrs. Taylor back from the hand, which, like a subterranean creature, balled up and flexed.

Please, Kent said. Start again. You were looking...

For a hospital, said Lucy, at last. One with different color rooms. Rooms to treat patients. A color for every illness. We're looking for a yellow one.

Kitty and Kent exchanged a look.

You've come, said Kent, to the right place.

He turned to Kitty.

See, he said. I knew we could help.

Helping is your greatest vice, Kitty said.

I don't understand, said Lucy.

What's to understand. You're looking for a hospital with different color rooms.

And you've found one, said Kitty.

Lucy looked around. The long hallway, it's aquamarine tiles, it's desk and doorways. It looked like any other hospital.

But it's not, said Lucy. This isn't...

She was flustered. It wasn't supposed to be like this. It either was or it wasn't. But this, with these two, everything seemed something else.

We're looking for a real hospital, she said.

This isn't real? Kitty said, with alarm.

Shhh, Kent said. Shhh. It's ok.

It's... Lucy tried again to figure out the word she meant.

Obsolete? Said Kent.

Iridescent, Kitty replied.

Decayed, Kent said firmly.

Opulent? Kitty offered.

Defunct, said Kent.

Out of business, Kitty said. Everything must go.

Hospitals don't do that, Lucy said. They don't...stop. She paused and thought of every hospital she knew.

Sure they do.

All the time.

Every day.

We should know.

We've been here forever.

And before that.

We used to come here as kids.

Years and years ago.

Do you remember?

It seems like yesterday.

Everything does.

We came to be *treated*.

The doctor said: Who's my mouse? Do you remember?

He didn't say that to *me*.

Who's my happy little mouse?

He always liked you more, Kitty pouted. Treated you better.

That's it, he said. Let it out.

She stuck out her tongue.

He tickled me when he said it. Who's my mouse? Who's my happy little mouse? And he would laugh and you and Mom would laugh and I laughed too, I even laughed, though I didn't want to. I didn't *want to* laugh. I didn't want to be a mouse. Who wants to be a mouse? His hands were so hot. So hot and coarse.

Our birth was difficult, Kitty explained. *His* was. Mine was easy, which tends to explain everything.

It's my job, he said, beating the unbroken path—it's my solemn duty as one of the elect. But anyway, I was saying, one day—I'll never forget it.

Kitty smirked.

He pulls me in and sits me down on the exam table and begins to tell me a story. He says, When I was your age I loved a girl who was very sick. Sicker than you by a large margin.

And then turned and walked down the hall a bit kicking papers up into the air.

Everyone in the neighborhood loved her, but I loved her the most. For her I would take pictures of things she couldn't see because she was so sick. Sunsets, kittens, the beautiful things that girls like. Because, you understand, he told me, she was confined to her room with sickness.

Kitty picked up two file folders, looked at them a moment, peered, studiously, and then began, slowly, to dance.

And I would bring them to her, these pictures, and hand them through the window. In return she would leave me notes of appreciation and, dare I say, reciprocation. In sum, he said, we were happy.

She held the files in front of her like fans and spasmodically affected a burlesque.

One day, however, he said, she left a note saying she wanted something new. Bring me a picture of a rotting bird carcass, the note said. I didn't know what a rotting bird carcass had to do with anything or why you would want one—I was young and stupid—but I did as she said. She was my one true love. I looked around until I found one. Killed by a cat, I imagine. I took the photo, had it developed and brought it to her. When I came back the next day, her note said: Even your pictures of death are beautiful. That was the last time I heard from her.

And as he's telling me this he's prepping a shot. He's holding the syringe and squirting liquid out of the needle with flourish.

From mouse to man, he said and jammed the needle into my arm.

Then rubbing gently where he jabbed he said, Our little secret.

Kitty stopped her dance and stared at Kent.

Never happened, she said, finally, and winked at Lucy and Mrs. Taylor.

But she couldn't really wink and instead scrunched up her face to do it.

What were we talking about? Kent asked.

The yellow room, Kitty said.

The yellow room, the boy said. The chamber within the chamber.

The secret sanctuary, said Kitty.

The slow escape, Kent rejoined.

Pressure wick catastrophe, Mrs. Taylor said, suddenly agitated.

Kent and Kitty considered them.

She's just fabulous, Kent said. Can we lick her?

What?

Lick her, kiss her, touch mouth to skin.

It's reverential, said Kitty. It's not weird.

Like disciples with the withered feet of a dead saint.

If you let us, we'll tell you what you want.

You want a room and we want a taste of the thing that brings us.

The boy's watched beeped.

Here my love, he said. Fancy time. And removed a pill, placing it gently onto her tongue.

Kitty closed her eyes and swallowed.

The yellow room, she said.

Mrs. Taylor stared straight ahead, her own head lolling back and forth on her neck, a buoy in troubled sea.

The room was up one more floor and down a few halls. Mrs. Taylor was silent. Her breathing was low and deep. More and more silent. They stopped in every room. Neon orange, taupe, umber, peach. Ruby, crimson, fire engine, rust, brick. Fern, forest, jungle, moss, tea—they would never find it. They would never find it because there was no such thing; the twins had lied; this wasn't the place; there was no place. But then finally, suddenly, there it was, yes at last, yellow. The room. She stood at the entrance with Mrs. Taylor. She stood on the threshold. Pale yellow. Palest. Hay. Last light on a cold day. They had found it. Lucy wheeled Mrs. Taylor in, positioning her to face the bed where Lucy could see her if she needed to. They had found their right place. She climbed into the bed and sat there, knees pulled to her chest. On the ceiling there were stains and a long crack. She thought about the orderly, the orderly and his mother. Would they miss her? she wondered. And when she returned to them would they know her? She looked over at Mrs. Taylor, who was already asleep. The sleep that is not yet sleep, the long walk into the always-snarling wind. She lay down and waited. Sleep that was not sleep, purity, transition—to become so heavy she could not get up again. She thought of the orderly and his mother around the kitchen table, their faces a mask of concern. The orderly over her, kissing her neck, sweat beading his brow. No, to not want to get up or even think of trying. There was a boy once, there was a girl once, there was a place for them. Soon it would come for her, the slow escape. Soon it would come. The orderly, his mother, her mother, the brother. They all held hands together in her head. They all sang for her. She waited and waited.

Meanwhile, in the hallway the siblings remained. Resumed.

The boy said, Let's start over.

The girl nodded.

Today I'm, she looked at the file. Oh, inoperable brain tumor.

I'm so sorry.

But I have so much to live for.

Please, go on.

I have a young wife and we're expecting a child.

A tricky situation. Delicate.

I'll never get to see her grow up.

Not necessarily.

To see her scrape her knee against the pavement.

Blood is a rite of the long egress.

To watch her lose her joy.

Things could be different, he said.

In what way, she said, warily.

Maybe the tumor doesn't kill you. Maybe it alters your personality so substantially that you are unrecognizable to the ones you love.

The girl bit her lip.

Maybe you can no longer love.

She shook her head back and forth.

You can remember loving but you can't feel love.

Her eyes glistened.

All you can do is play at loving.

When Lucy finally got back to the house—maybe it was days later—after she had woke and found herself still in the dingy hospital, sunless light revealing the room—not really the right color yellow after all—and Mrs. Taylor asleep, unwaking, no words, no groans, just breath after breath, and drove her back to the Chateau, leaving her there on the pavement, curled into the chair, nestled, a kiss on the cheek, and the keys in the van parked there on the curb, the phone was already ringing. For a while she ignored it. Then she called out to the mother. Finally, she steeled herself and picked it up.

I've been thinking about you, the voice said. I've been sitting here and thinking about your eyes. I've been calling for hours.

It was the orderly.

Where's here? she said.

A place of magic and possible redemption, the orderly said.

Are you sick? she asked. Are you in the hospital?

He laughed. It was a sharp and startled laugh.

My love, my love, he said. Then he gave her directions.

Come for dinner, he said before hanging up. And don't tell my mother.

The orderly's directions were uncharacteristic. They included stopping at certain places and looking at certain things. For example, she was supposed to stop at a man-made lake in a park and look at the ducks in the pond. *Notice their serenity,* the directions read. However, by the time she got to the park, there were no ducks in the pond. There was only a guy sitting on a bench and staring and rubbing his thighs. She was also supposed to stop a house and look carefully into the picture window, notice a billboard above a convenience store, and count the number of flowers in a flowerbed. She decided not to do any of these things. The orderly would tell her all about them anyway. He would stand there and impart. By the time she was, as she understood it, halfway there, she threw the directions away. She suddenly understood where she was going.

When she got there it was dark. The gate to the development was closed but the light in the security booth was on. In it, Belvedere sat reading. He seemed deeply engrossed in his book. She walked right up to the booth and knocked on the glass. Belvedere started. He was wearing a tube in his nose. The tube was connected to a tank.

Hi Belvedere, she said.

Who the hell are you? Belvedere grumbled.

Belvedere, she said. It's me.

Who?

Me, she said. She moved closer to the booth.

He studied her with concentration. Then he smiled a little.

I know you, he said, wrinkling his already wrinkled brow. You're…

I'm the girl who lost the dog, she offered.

The girl who lost the dog, he repeated.

Did you ever find it? he asked.

No, she said.

That's sad, Belvedere said a bit absently

The tank attached to Belvedere made an erratic sound that was something between a clock ticking and gas escaping some vacuum. It sounded like a dying metronome.

But she was found, she said. The dog. Eventually she was found.

Well, that's great, Belvedere interjected gently.

Just not by me, she finished.

Dogs are fickle, Belvedere said. They're like wives in that way. You think they're happy just sitting there in their chairs. You think they're content. But one day you find out different. One day you find out that in fact all along they've been plotting ways to follow their passions. They're *scheming*. It reminds me of a poem I once read.

Oh, said Lucy.

I have a hard time remembering it, though, Belvedere said.

Ok, she said.

Lucy stood there with him for a moment, not knowing whether or how to leave. Belvedere sat in the booth. He did not return to his book and he did not continue the conversation. He stared past her into the night. Shhft. Shhft. Shhft, said the machine attached to him.

She turned to go.

He seems to me a dog that dog, Belvedere said.

What? she said, turning back around.

That's how the poem starts, said Belvedere.

Oh, she said.

Do you like it? he asked.

Well, she began.

You don't like it, he said, sadly.

I don't know if I like it, she said. How can I tell if I like it when I've only heard the first line?

That's hogwash, Belvedere said, getting agitated. You know you like a flavor of ice cream after just the first lick.

I'm not sure a poem is like ice cream.

Bullshit! Belvedere said, getting even more agitated. How is a poem *not* like ice cream?

For a moment, neither spoke. Belvedere was wheezing and his machine was ticking away.

It's a nice line, though, she said to him. It's a good start.

I'm glad you like it, Belvedere wheezed. It's so hard to like anything these days. When you find something that grabs you, you should try to remember exactly what it is.

The house where the orderly was looked exactly like the house she had once peered into. Maybe it was the same house. It was hard to say. As she entered, the orderly called out to her. Lucy followed his voice to the dining room, which was fully decorated and tastefully lit. The orderly was sitting at the table. On it he had placed platters with chicken breasts, mashed potatoes, evenly diced carrots, and a bottle of wine. The setting was for two. The orderly made a gesture for her to sit down. He smiled a slight but satisfied smile.

You came! he said.

You asked me to, she said.

I'm glad you came, he said. I'm not gonna lie. For a while I was worried.

It doesn't look like you were worried, she said.

Worry can take many forms, the orderly said.

He was wearing a grey slacks and a navy sweater over a crisp white-collared shirt. His hair had been parted and brushed across his head. He smelled of wild flowers and leather. He seemed scrubbed clean of any nasty particulars. He looked like a photograph.

Here, he said. He placed one of the chicken breasts and some vegetables on her plate.

She looked at the food. The chicken breast looked rubbery and the vegetables soft.

I'm not really hungry, she said.

Of course you are, he said. You probably just don't know what you're hungry for. Besides it would really mean a lot to me. To have you help me do my job. It would mean a lot.

Your job? she said.

Mmmhmm, he said, his mouth full of chicken.

I don't understand, she said.

This is what I do, he said. This is my job. This.

He waved his arm around as if he was showcasing goods.

I thought your job was to sell houses, she said.

Homes, he corrected. To sell homes.

He paused to take a bite of the chicken. He closed his eyes while he did.

Anyone can sell a house, he said, while still chewing. But in order to sell a home, you have to make it feel like a home. Here, he said. Taste this.

He held a fork in front of Lucy's face. He held it there until she opened her mouth.

It has to feel loved, he said. Caressed. You can't fake something like that. You can't simulate the feeling of home. That's good, right? I knew you were hungry.

Lucy chewed on her chicken. It wasn't good. But it wasn't bad either. It tasted maybe a little like the idea of chicken.

You're living here, she said, after she finished chewing.

Not just here, he said, brightly. I move from place to place. I'm the closer for the company. It took me a while to really believe it. I mean, who really ever thinks their number will be called? But when they desperately need to sell something, they call me in.

He put his hand on top of her hand. It was cool and dry.

I have a quality. That's what Steve says.

Steve? she said.

My boss, he said.

A quality? she said.

To have a quality is a rare thing. Anyone can sell a house, but it takes a quality to transform a house into a home. That's what Steve says.

The dining room was painted steel gray and decorated with ornate empty white frames of different sizes. They practically covered the walls. To her it seemed like they were each waiting for a picture: for a face, or several faces, for a body, or several bodies, a landscape, a smile, a deathly tableau. To her they looked like a bunch of eyes fixing her in their indiscriminant stare. Too many eyes.

Chicken means home, the orderly said. Cookies also mean home, he continued. Food in general, you know. It activates primal memories. The family, the hearth, the willed emotional bastion against the bewildering darkness. Everyone feels it. It's why all parties inevitably end up in the kitchen.

Across from her, above a burnished sideboard was an oval mirror. In it she watched herself as the orderly explained his transformations.

But chicken is especially good. You need a little blood to make a home. A little sacrifice. It reminds people of their childhood.

The girl in the mirror nodded uncertainly.

The important thing is it can't be too specific, the orderly said. No sauerkraut, no fish. No exotic spices or regional favorites. In times of uncertainty people want their dreams to be part of larger dream. Something they already know and understand. A broad canvas of which their only responsibility is one tiny corner.

Lucy recalled once finding a half of a photograph. In it a plump woman posed seductively on a bed. The woman sat on the edge of the bed; she sat with her weight on her left hip and her legs were curled next to her. Her hands were clasped behind her head and her chest thrust out and up. She was wearing a black satin nightie, kind of translucent and cut low in the neckline. The room that the woman posed in was dimly lit and both sufficiently organized and somehow dirty. It might have been a motel room. Behind the woman was a half-opened bureau. In this half of the photograph, you could only see the bureau's door, ajar. It was mirrored and reflected obliquely the back of the woman. Her hair was messy and her back had several large moles. You could not, in this half of the photograph, tell what was in the bureau. You could not see what memory someone had decided to keep in favor of this woman, who, on her own half of the photograph, was trying so very hard.

The vessel, the orderly said, must be empty. But it's got to be a recognizable vessel.

After dinner, he showed her around. They walked from room to room. The house had an open floor plan. It had wood floors and granite counter tops. It was spacious and clean and gave the impression of circumscribed possibility. These were all good things, the orderly assured her.

In the master bedroom, complete with walk-in closet and his-and-her bathroom sinks, he kissed her neck. He stood behind her, pressing himself onto her, and wrapped his arms around her waist. She could feel his expectation envelop her. This could be us, he said to her. This could be our life.

She tried to imagine their life. In this capacious and luxurious room, they seemed like children. They also seemed like impostors. They were waiting, she knew, to be recognized, to be scooped up by some giant chastising hand.

Here? she said, skeptically.

This place, another place, the orderly said. There is no limit to the horizon.

The horizon is the limit, she said, softly. It's the unreachable thing, she thought.

He kissed her neck again. This time his tongue darted out from between his teeth and he gently licked her.

We could take our parts in the great parade, the orderly said. We could plug ourselves right into the circuit.

It was hard to imagine, this life, its contours and furniture. There was no mirror in the bedroom to help her.

What about your mother? she asked.

He squeezed her tightly.

Mothers get left behind, he said. Every single day. It's how you know they're really mothers.

That night the orderly undressed her. He took off her clothes one piece at a time, removing each with a dramatic flourish and tossing it carelessly aside. He tried to make sultry eye contact with her each time, as if slipping off her shoe or yanking her jeans down to her ankles was supposed to excite her beyond measure. While he did this, Lucy did not look at him. Instead she looked around the bedroom. It looked like the bedroom of people who thought a lot about what is like to be in a bedroom. When he had finished and she was standing there in that strange room in only her underwear, he too undressed. His divestment was more hurried, though. It was anxious. He hopped around on one foot pulling off his shoes and at his socks.

Then they both stood there. His body looked thin. Did it always look thin? It looked thinner than usual, then. On the bed, he put his hands all over her. They were not tender. Instead they felt diligent and tense. They maneuvered her around the bed for a little bit. His hand, his arms. They nudged her into place. She wanted to like it or at least to give the impression that she liked it, but all she felt was the coldness of the air conditioning and strangeness of the room and it was hard to concentrate, or not concentrate, or whatever it was that would make it better but it wasn't. Once he had said to her: let's try it where I pretend to be a spider and kind of squatted on his hand and feet and hopped around a little bit and she had laughed because she though he was joking but he wasn't joking and got upset and sat there sulking, naked, on the bed, so, in the end they tried it, just to make him feel better, but still it was weird and didn't go very well. She felt a little bit like that now.

Afterwards for a while Lucy slept. Did she dream? It was hard to remember. Certain dreams are not like dreams at all. They are more like glimpses into the world without you in it. A room, a phone, a small around table, two people. Was she one? The orderly woke her with a shake.

Hey, he said. Hey.

He gave her a kindly smile.

You can't stay here, he said.

What? she said. She thought she misheard him.

The night, he said. You can't stay the night. It's not good for the house.

His face was full of earnest concern.

People want their homes to be free from sin, he said.

What? she said again.

His face was full of earnest concern; it was a postcard from some terrible vacation.

I'm sure you understand, he said and kissed her on the forehead.

236

Lucy walked home the same way she had come. The night had become cold and empty. She passed by Belvedere sleeping in his booth. She passed by houses and cars, comatose and still. She hugged herself a little and rubbed her arms.

Ahead of her a bus was idling. She ran up to it and knocked on the door.

The bus driver opened the door and welcomed her into the bus.

What's a young lady like you doin' out so late? he said.

She shrugged.

Dead girls tell no tales, huh.

The only other person on the bus was a plump woman with a riot of orange ringlet curls. For some time she was silent. The only sound was the sound of the bus idling. Plus the bus driver. He hummed a little tune. It was as if he too was waiting for the bus to start, as if the behemoth would suddenly rear up and lumber forward and his job was to merely direct it, to manage it, as best he could. He seemed content to do this, happy in his vigilance.

Suddenly the woman with the orange curls sat up

straight and said loudly: You gonna *tell* me when we get to Teller street.

Yes, Ma'am, the bus driver replied.

You told me you were gonna tell me when get to Teller street, the woman said.

You can't miss Teller street, the bus driver said. There's a store with a big cartoon bear holding a mop. All lit up.

I'm getting' out of a bad relationship, the woman said.

Well, we'll get you there, the bus driver said. We'll help you out.

Oh no! the woman said, emphatically. *You* can't help me. No *man* gonna help *me out*. Ain't nobody can help me but Jesus, she said, shaking her head.

We'll get you to your destination, the bus driver said. Is all I meant.

I don't even know my own destination, the woman with the curls replied with agitation. I've been livin' too long in the flesh. I'm getting' out a bad relationship. I've been livin' too long in the flesh. But I'm *tryin'* to live in the spirit.

The bus driver ignored her. He started up the bus. The woman sank back into her seat and sang softly to herself. Lucy leaned her head against the window. The bus snaked its way through the sprawling streets. The view from the window was occluded by steam and dirt. She could just barely make out the neighborhoods they were passing through, the squat buildings, the spindly trees, but still they passed through them, the neighborhoods, through the trees and by the houses and shops, they passed through them slowly but without care, without attention; inside the houses, the buildings, the shops, the people slept, cold, indifferent, submerged in the black waters of their own helpless dreaming. The orderly too was dreaming. In the strange bedroom he sprawled on the large bed and descended. As did the mother in her cluttered room and Mrs. Taylor—she too—dormant in her antiseptic cell: they both slept; they both dreamt. But what did it matter? Everyone dreams and everyone wakes. They leave the bramble but they do not carry it with them. They don't notice the scratches and the cuts. The orderly didn't notice. No. He never noticed. He never noticed because he had plans. Because he was going to arrange their lives into necessary patterns; assemble them into colors and shapes. He didn't care for brambles or forests. He didn't understand the hospital and its promises, the real hospital, which was even now still out there, still, somewhere, somewhere, waiting for her, calling her, leading her home.

The woman with the curls sang softly to herself and her song was a song about bones. Lucy closed her eyes and opened them. The bus stopped and started again. Through the windows she could see, but barely, the bleary halo of the streetlights. They beckoned to the bus with their ghostly arms. When she was little this was how she thought of them, the streetlights; she thought that they were sentinels, guardians, and the long, orange shafts of light were their arms, their long arms reaching out to usher along the traveling cars, passing each one to another, gently, patiently, carrying them safely home. In the backseat of the car, in the darkness she would peer out at the streetlights and squint. Squinting made the arms longer, extending their reach. In the darkness she sat and waited for the next arm to reach her. The arms reached out, the stately arms. She alone understood their secret.

Acknowledgments

The foregoing would not have been possible without the intelligence, generosity, and support of many people. Martin Riker, Danielle Dutton, Laird Hunt, and Selah Saterstrom graced this book and with their keen eyes and brilliant minds and made it better; Julie Doxsee, J'Lyn Chapman, and Sara Veglahn opened their ears and hearts too many times to count; Christina Mengert, Paul Fattaruso, Brian Kiteley, Eleni Sikelianos, and Bin Ramke offered alternate visions, support, and ways of being; Curtis White gave me the tools and the path; Jeffrey DeShell took the project on and believed in it; Scott Fitzgerald, Ivanna Bergese, Christina Dirks, Marc Willwerth, Sarah Gaudette, Kim Percival, and Naomi Roth—family always; Kathy Bernau, Edwin Bernau II, and the rest of the Bernau clan, in particular Edwin J. Bernau (in memoriam); Beverly Fiegel; Mel, Mary Jo, and Elizabeth Howard; and most of all—in perpetual awe and gratitude—Heather. Thank you.

Portions of Hospice have appeared in altered forms in *NOÖ Journal*, *Harp and Altar*, and *Trickhouse*. My gratitude to Mike Young, Keith Newton, and Noah Saterstrom for their guidance and curation.